STRANGERS

Published in the United States of America by
CRYSTAL INK Publishing
Indianapolis, Indiana

First Edition

ISBN: 978-0971958678

Cover Art by Judy Bullard of Custom Ebook

STRANGERS

by

Crystal V. Rhodes

CRYSTAL INK Publishing
Indianapolis, Indiana

DEDICATION

This book is dedicated to those friends and family members who have encouraged me from the beginning to follow my passion. It is also dedicated to the readers whose loyalty has been my inspiration to continue to follow my dream.

ACKNOWLEDGEMENTS

I want to thank Eunice, Mel, Ezeral, Shirley, Babette and Keesha. Each of you has meant so much to the development of this work. I am grateful.

NOVELS
by
Crystal V. Rhodes

Romantic Suspense

Sin
Sweet Sacrifice
Sinful Intentions
Singing a Song
Small Sensations
Stillwaters
Secrets
Strangers
Shadows of Love

The Stillwaters Series

Someone Like Me
Someone Like You
Someone Like Them

Cozy Mysteries
by
L. Barnett Evans and C.V. Rhodes

Grandmothers, Incorporated
Saving Sin City
There's Something Wrong with Miss Zelda
Whose Knife is it Anyway?

All books are available in Ebook and Paperback format

STRANGERS

PROLOGUE

As he sat in the corner of the tiny structure that served as a café and gossip center, the man sipped his cup of coffee, lazily, while reading the newspaper. He sat alone with his back to the wall, facing the dozen or so wood-hued tables and chairs occupying the minute space.

He was friendly enough, nodding and smiling at his neighbors who drifted in and out of the building. His fellow islanders greeted him in return, but they respected his privacy. Rarely did he include himself in conversation or gossip. Years ago he had appeared among them as a tourist, and stayed to establish himself as a resident. Still, he remained a stranger among them.

Since the day of his arrival on the island he would come into the café and order a cup of coffee and a breakfast roll. He would then wander to a bin where an assortment of old newspapers were stacked, sort through them, withdraw one, and then sit at his favorite table where he would sip, eat and read. The newspapers were usually left in the café by tourists, but he didn't seem to mind that some had been there so long they had yellowed from age. He read each page meticulously, his actions so perfectly timed that he completed his coffee and roll the same instant that he finished reading. Afterward, he'd neatly fold the paper, take a writing pen from his pocket and put a mark on the front of the issue so that he wouldn't withdraw the same newspaper from the bin again. This had been the man's routine for years. It never varied—until today.

The café owner was caught off-guard when the man stood so suddenly that he knocked the coffee cup off of the table. The earthen mug fell to the floor, shattering into pieces. Startled, the owner looked up in time to see the look of shocked disbelief on the man's face as he stared at the newspaper page in his hand. Before the owner could get to the table to clean up the thick dark liquid seeping into the worn wooden floor boards, the man had rushed out of the building carrying the newspaper page in his hand. He hadn't finished his roll, nor had he read the rest of the paper. He also got to leave the generous tip that he always left.

Resigned, the owner gathered the remaining sections of the newspaper and wondered what could have possibility caused the man to leave so unexpectedly. Glancing at the masthead of the newspaper pages left behind, he noted that this particular edition was a few years old and was some entertainment publication called *Variety*.

CHAPTER 1

Dana Mansfield was close to hyperventilating. She had to get a hold of herself before she passed out. Her body was trembling and she tried hard to pull herself together as she made an attempt to understand what was happening. First, there had been the telephone call and then—

"Hello?"

Dana jumped. The voice was deep and masculine and it was coming from the waiting room which she thought was deserted. Her mind raced. Her eyes shifted toward the open doorway *Who could that be?* She hadn't been expecting anybody. The staff had gone for the day and she was here alone, or so she thought. Could it be the caller? Her first impulse was to rush to the door, close and lock it, but it was too late as the voice suddenly materialized into the shape of a figure blocking the doorway.

The man was tall—very tall—at least six feet six, with a muscular build. He was dressed casually in blue jeans, a t-shirt and sneakers. Some sort of tattoo adorned the bulging muscle beneath his t-shirt sleeve. His complexion was golden brown. His head was shaved bald. He sported a neatly trimmed goatee and he wore sunglasses. His persona certainly didn't calm the anxiety that she was feeling. He could be the stranger who had called.

"I didn't mean to scare you," he told her, reacting to her fearful eyes meeting his shaded ones. "The office door was unlocked and nobody was at the receptionist's desk. I called out, but there was no answer—" He stopped short.

The demeanor of the attractive woman staring back at him put him on instant alert. She appeared shaken.

"Is that the package?" Dana asked sharply, glancing at the small parcel in his hand. It was wrapped in brown paper and tied with string. The man looked down at the box.

"Uh, yeah, I guess so," he said vaguely. He held it out to her.

"What's in it?" Dana didn't take her eyes off of him.

He shrugged. "How should I know?"

"Well, you brought it in here," she snapped. How dare this man stand there and act as though he didn't know what was happening.

"Listen lady, I don't know what your problem is, but all I want to do is drop off a key. When I was in the hall I saw this package in front of the door, picked it up and came inside."

Placing the neatly wrapped bundle on the desk, he reached into his pocket and withdrew a door key. He slammed it down next to the package.

"Now here's the key. Give me my deposit check and I'm outta here." He returned her insolent glare.

Dana gave the abandoned key a cursory glance before returning her attention to him.

"I don't know what you're talking about! What key? What deposit? What are you saying? Are you asking for the ransom right now?"

"Whoa!" The man took a step backward with both hands held up as if to ward off a blow. "Ransom? What ransom? Let's start over here. I'm James Starr, Mrs. Mansfield…"

"How do you know my name?" Dana's voice bristled with suspicion.

"I've seen a picture of you with your niece," he replied, referring to singing superstar, Darnell Cameron. "I've also read that you're her attorney. Plus, your brother-in-law, Ray Wilson. is a friend of mine."

He was also aware that Ray was Darnell's stepfather. Yet, the mention of Ray's name drew no reaction from the woman. He persisted.

"I'm the guy who rented your condo. I got your place through Ray."

Dana looked at him blankly, trying to reconcile what he was saying with the reality of what she was presently facing. She vaguely remembered that her older sister, Bev, had made arrangements for the rental of Dana's L.A. condo while Dana was away at her family's home recuperating from an accident.

"So you're not one of them?"

"No, I guess I'm not," James answered, disturbed by the question. "But who are you talking about when you say *them*?" His suspicions were rising. He hoped that what he was thinking was wrong.

Dana didn't answer as she walked away from him. James noticed that the fear in her eyes was still there.

"Ray's friend," she mumbled as if trying to process what he was saying. "Yes, I remember. Bev told me something about you." She whirled to face him. "You're the guy from New York City."

"Yes." James was relieved that she seemed more rational. "I moved to L.A. a while ago and..."

"Aren't you a cop?" Dana looked wary.

"Not anymore. I'm a partner in a security firm now."

"A security firm...a security firm," Dana repeated absently. She was finding it hard to focus. All she could think about was the telephone call that she had received.

Withdrawing his wallet from his back pocket, he pulled a business card from its interior and handed it to her. Dana glimpsed at the card but didn't take it.

"Business has been good in L.A.," James continued. "We're expanding to Northern California. I'm headed to San Francisco today to open a second West Coast office. I called earlier and told the woman I spoke to that I would drop off the key to the condo. She said my deposit would be here and—"

James' voice drifted off. Dana wasn't listening. Her eyes were fixed on the package that he had placed on her desk.

Returning the card to his wallet, James gave a frustrated sigh. *Oh hell! What have I stepped into?*

He had been a cop for over twenty years and was familiar with the look on this woman's face. Dana Mansfield was terrified, and his presence in her office wasn't the reason. He hadn't missed the word "ransom" in their conversation and there was this package wrapped in brown paper that seemed to be causing her distress. Toss in the fact that she was a high class attorney, with a rich and famous client, and even a rookie could read between the lines of what was happening here.

"Mrs. Mansfield," he said as a pair of sad eyes looked up at him. "Has somebody that you know been kidnapped?"

****

In California, in the picturesque town of Carmel-by-the Sea, Mrs. Sharon, the housekeeper for the Stewart family, pulled into the garage of the multi-million dollar home in which she was employed. Glancing at her watch, she checked the time, hoping that her trip to the store hadn't cut into the extra time she needed to fix the meal that her employer, actor, Thad Stewart, had requested. He and his wife, Darnell, were returning home after having been gone for a week. He had called Mrs. Sharon and asked her to make his favorite meal to celebrate their return. Tonight was special. They had been away from their daughter, Nia, for much too long and the reunion would be a joyous one. The five-year-old was now enrolled in kindergarten and was no longer traveling with her parents.

While they were gone Nia was staying with Darnell's half brother, Sinclair Reasoner, and his wife, Nedra. The Reasoner family lived down the street. However, Mrs. Sharon had been picking Nia up at school this week, along with her cousin, Gillian. But, Thad called earlier and informed her that a limo was being sent to the school for his daughter in celebration of her parents' returning home. The news had given the housekeeper extra time to go to the grocery store and to fix the welcome home meal.

Taking the groceries out of the trunk, she could hear the telephone ringing in the house. Hurrying inside, she placed the grocery bag on the island counter and raced to answer the call. The ringing stopped before she reach the telephone. Caller I.D. read Nedra Davis-Reasoner.

"She probably wants to know if the Stewarts are home yet," Mrs. Sharon muttered aloud. "I'll give her a call back later."

At the moment, she had too much to do.

CHAPTER 2

"I received a call on my office telephone," Dana relayed to this stranger who had walked into her life so unexpectedly. "The voice was distorted but he said that I would receive a package proving that my great niece, Nia, and my young cousin, Gillian, had been kidnapped. Of course when you walked in…"

"You thought I was delivering the package," James concluded.

Dana nodded, wondering if she had sealed her loved ones fate by having told him a narrative that she wasn't suppose to reveal. But since he had been a police officer maybe he had some sort of solution to this dilemma.

"You say that Nia is your great-niece?" There was an unspoken question in James' inquiry. Dana knew what he was asking.

"She's Darnell and Thad Stewart's daughter." That simple statement explained why the child was abducted. The celebrity couple was one of the wealthiest in the entertainment industry. "Gillian Reasoner is Darnell's brother's child. Her parents are wealthy too."

She began to pace back and forth aimlessly while James watched her restless movements. He couldn't help but note that Dana Mansfield was an attractive woman.

He would guess her to be about 5 feet 4 inches tall and her age to be somewhere in her late thirties. She was slender, but there were curves evident beneath the finely tailored skirt suit that she wore. Its vibrant color was complemented by her cocoa brown complexion. Her oval shaped face was framed by a short haircut, and perfectly arched eyebrows enhanced her dark brown eyes. Full lips were accented with rose colored lipstick, and at the moment those lips were tight with anguish.

Dana felt trapped between a rock and a hard place. She had the lives of two innocent children in her hands and she didn't know which way to turn. She stopped pacing and fixed James with a apprehensive glare.

"You're not going to the authorities are you?" Dana wanted to kick herself for having said anything to this man. What had she been thinking?

"If you didn't want me to then why did you tell me?"

Dana wondered why herself? The words seemed to have tumbled from her lips without rhyme or reason. She could think of only one explanation.

"Well, you are an ex-cop."

"And?" he prompted.

"And I'm not sure what to do. I had to tell somebody." She felt like a balloon filled with helium and was about to burst.

Turning away from his watchful gaze, her attention returned to the package. James read her mind.

"You're wondering what's in it, but I would advise you to handle it with care. There might be fingerprints and they could prove valuable."

Dana nodded in understanding, but made no move toward the package. Fear of what she might find inside kept her frozen in place. James came to her rescue.

"I'll open it if you don't mind."

Dana was grateful that he offered. She watched with curiosity as he carefully took a pencil and removed the string holding the brown wrapping paper in place. The ends weren't taped and it fell easily from the small cardboard box. There was no tape on the top of the box.

Using the pencil he lifted one flap and then the other. The pencil disappeared inside the box and came back up with the handles of a brightly colored child size purse dangling from its end. Dana's breath caught in her throat.

"That's Nia's purse. My sister, Bev, bought it for her. She carries it everywhere she goes."

Wrapping her arms around her torso, Dana gave an agonizing groan. Her eyes filled with tears that she refused to shed. Reason was needed if she wanted to get through this, and her first hurdle would be a big one.

"How am I going to tell Darnell and Thad?" Her hand flew to her mouth in distress. "Oh Lord! And Gillian's parents! I've got to tell them too."

"You're on overload. Take a deep breath and try to focus, " James urged.

There was a quiet authority in the man's voice that caught Dana's attention. He took a seat across from her desk, crossed his muscled arms, and placed his ankle across his knee. While Dana's mind was trying frantically to charge through a tornado, he looked as though he was romping on a sandy beach. James was calm, cool and collected. Why shouldn't he be? The lives at stake meant nothing to him. She should have never told him what was happening and was starting to regret having confided in him. Maybe if he left her office, he might forget all about the situation and not say anything to anyone. She had her doubts that would happen, and nearly snorted aloud at the thought. Yet, it was worth a try.

"Listen, Mr. Starr. This is not your problem. I shouldn't have involved you in the first place. All I ask is that when you leave here you don't mention this to anyone."

James looked at her steadily. He understood her fear and anxiety, but there was a reality to face.

"Lady, you're a lawyer so you know that kidnapping is a federal offense. Maybe you don't want to hear this, but the best advice I can give you is that you need to call the authorities."

He was right. Dana didn't want to hear it. Her voice was steel.

"I haven't called the parents of these children yet. My family has got to know what's happening first. They have to make the decision where to go from there."

Dismissively, she turned away from him, walked to her desk and picked up the telephone.

Looking at her rigid back, James stood to leave. This was none of his business. He was heading north today to open a new office. He had to find a place to live and hire a staff. His list of priorities was endless. He didn't have time to get involved with some kidnapping. It was obvious that the woman was stubborn and was going to do what she wanted. The best thing for him to do was to walk out of the door and never look back. Still, there were two little girls out there somewhere and they were in danger. How could he walk away? With that thought in mind, James sat back down in Dana's office and waited.

****

The tiny room was dim. There were no windows. A goose neck lamp sitting on the floor beside a single twin size mattress provided the only light. An air vent was in the ceiling, but it wasn't allowing much air to penetrate. The room was hot and stuffy and getting more uncomfortable with each passing minute.

Gillian Reasoner's dark brown eyes took in every detail of the room as she slowly surveyed the surroundings in which she and Nia Cameron Stewart were imprisoned. The walls were gray and the paint was peeling. The plastic was still on the twin size mattress on which Nia and she reclined, but no sheets had been provided. There was only one pillow and it had no pillow case.

The door leading out of the room wasn't new. It was old and made of heavy wood. The door knob was removed, and the hole where the knob should have been was covered with a piece of wood. The door was locked from the outside. Gillian couldn't help but wonder what kind of lock it was. There was a doggy door at the bottom of the wooden structure, but it was only big enough for a very small dog to get through. It looked as though it had been recently installed.

A short while ago, Nia and she watched as a tray of food was slipped through the doggy door. That had been after they both recovered from the horrible smelling substance that had rendered them unconscious. They didn't know how long they had been locked in the room, but they wanted out.

The door was too heavy for two young girls to knock down, but that doggy door— Gillian's eyes returned to the small square opening. It was hinged from the top and swung in and out. Common sense told her that the small door wouldn't have been there if they thought a kid could get through it, but that didn't mean she couldn't try. After all, she was to blame for them getting into the limo and being in this situation. She was mad enough to spit nails!

She should have known something was fishy when the chauffer drove up to the school and informed the teacher on dismissal duty that Nia's parents had sent the limo for her as a surprise. Mrs. Sharon picked them up every day, and Gillian knew that the housekeeper would have called the school and informed them of any change. Yet getting limo service was exciting, and the reason the chauffer gave for being there made sense.

The dismissal teacher had questioned the change in procedure, but the chauffer presented a letter of authorization on the limo company's letterhead. It was signed by Darnell Cameron Stewart. The signature was verified by school records.

It had been Gillian's enthusiastic endorsement of the arrangements that had put the girls inside the limo. The driver tried to prevent Gillian from coming, insisting that the directive was only for Nia. An indignant Gillian explained that if she didn't go, Nia wasn't going. Those words sealed both of their fates.

The girls hopped inside the limo happily, feeling important as they drove away from the school. It was when the driver made a turn off the highway in an area that Gillian didn't recognize that she started to ask questions. He told her that he needed to stop the car and adjust their seat belts.

Getting out of the limo he opened the back door and as soon as Gillian started to tell him that her belt didn't need adjusting he silenced her with a cloth over her nose and mouth. The next thing she knew Nia and she had awakened in this room.

Her cousin's large eyes were now looking at her in confusion, but she wasn't whimpering or crying. Gillian was proud of her because she knew that the little girl was scared. She was too, but right now anger was the stronger emotion.

She had tried to fit Nia through the doggy door, but as young as she was her body was still too large to get through it. As Gillian looked around their tiny prison, she knew that getting them out of this mess was her responsibility. For the first time in her life she was actually glad that she was small for her age. She would be twelve years old soon and she wasn't as tall as her Aunt Carla's ten year old twins, but her petite size might work to her advantage if she planned to get them out of here through the doggy door. Right now she couldn't figure another way out.

"I'm hungry."

Nia's voice interrupted her thoughts. Gillian gave her hand a reassuring squeeze, glad that she could do something immediate regarding that particular predicament. She picked up the tray and took it over to the mattress, placing it between them. It contained two sandwiches from a fast food restaurant. There were also two bags of potato chips and two sodas. Nia dug into her bag of chips first. Meanwhile, Gillian examined the silverware. Too bad the knife was plastic because if it had been metal she might have used it to help them escape. She could have sharpened it and tried to hurt whoever had taken them, or maybe—

While Nia dug into her sandwich, Gillian returned her attention to their present dilemma. Rising from the mattress she fell to her knees at the doggy door and listened closely for sounds. Hearing none, she pushed the small wooden door out a bit, and then a bit more. When it was wide enough she lay on her belly and stuck her head out of the doggy door as far as it could go. There was nothing to see but an empty hallway.

Gillian pulled her head back through the opening. She sat back on her haunches and studied the doggy door again.

Turning on her back she eased her head through the opening one more time. Her undertaking didn't take long this time, but she did observe that there was a latch lock keeping them locked inside the room. When she pulled her head back into the room the second time she studied the doggy door for so long that Nia finally broke the silence.

"Can we go home?"

Her inquiry sounded so hopeful that Gillian wanted to cry. She was aware that Nia didn't understand why they were in this strange place, sleeping on a mattress. She had asked Gillian was it a game. Gillian had to explain that the limo driver who brought them there did no without the permission of their parents, who didn't know where they were. She knew that her words scared Nia, but the little girl didn't cry. She wanted to be thought of as a big girl.

Gillian returned to the mattress and sat back down beside Nia. Pushing the tray aside, she gently placed her hands on the little girl's shoulders.

As they faced each other, Nia knew that something important was about to be said. She wanted her Mommy and Daddy, but since Gillian was with her she wasn't as scared as she would have been alone. Her cousin had told her that everything was going to be all right and she believed her. There was practically nothing that Gillian didn't know and couldn't do, so she turned trusting eyes to her waiting for her directions.

"We're strong girls," Gillian told her. "And we're from a strong and brave family."

Nia nodded. Every child in the large, extended Stillwaters clan had heard those words before.

"These are bad people who put us in here," Gillian declared. "But if they think we're going to stay they've got another think coming."

Nia nodded with fervor this time, certain that every word spoken was true.

"We're getting out of here!" Gillian exclaimed with determination.

Nia's eyes widened. *When? How?* Her cousin had the answer.

"This is what we're going to do."

CHAPTER 3

Dana wanted to tell her niece, nephew and cousins face to face what was happening, but there was no time to do that. Darnell and Thad should be on the Peninsula by now headed for home from their business trip. Nedra and Sin would both be leaving work soon and when they arrived home they would find that the girls weren't there.

After the call from the kidnapper she called the Reasoner household. Their housekeeper, Mrs. Lucia, informed Dana that the girls were late and that she assumed that Mrs. Sharon might have stopped to run an errand before bringing them home. That had happened before. Dana had shared that information with James Starr.

The kidnappers hadn't made a follow-up call and she wasn't sure what to do. The events of the day had Dana's errant emotions in disarray. She couldn't think straight. It seemed that this stranger, who she didn't know an hour ago, was thinking more clearly than she was as he offered her counsel.

"The FBI has the expertise to track those girls down and to keep this whole thing out of the media. That's another reason that you should call them. I'm sure that you don't want this to get out."

Dana recoiled at the idea. They both knew that a leak to the press could put the girls in greater danger.

"But I've got to tell their parents before I do anything. Like I said, it's really their decision, not mine."

James nodded in agreement. "Then you need to make that call now. You don't have any time to waste."

****

Sinclair Reasoner pulled up to the tall iron gate that had been added years ago to protect the privacy of the residents on their exclusive cul de sac. His half sister, Darnell Cameron and her husband, Thad, had financed its construction and upkeep. When the celebrity couple married, they wanted to assure that the quiet anonymity their neighbors enjoyed before the two superstars took up residence would continue.

Punching in the number code, he glided his luxury automobile past the five exquisite structures that dominated this idyllic setting. The architectural diversity of the houses ranged from California traditional to the ultra modern house in which his family lived. Each home was set back from the street by a sea of perfectly manicured lawns. Only one house couldn't be seen from the street. The Stewart home was set apart from the others by a high gated wall.

As he passed their place he thought about Mrs. Sharon. He was grateful for her assistance in picking up the children at school. Usually, he or his wife did pickup duty, but things were hectic at work this week for both of them. Neither was able to do the job. Their own housekeeper, Mrs. Lucia, stayed with the girls until Nedra or he arrived home.

At the end of their lengthy driveway, Sin jumped out of his vehicle to look into the mailbox. It was empty. Hopping back into the car he hoped that Nedra was home. If the girls were preoccupied, maybe he and his wife might be able to get in a little quickie. He smiled at the thought.

Nedra Davis Reasoner watched from a window in the living room as her husband drove toward their house. He couldn't get there fast enough. She was frantic.

When she arrived home she knew that their fifteen year old son, Trevor, wouldn't be there. He was on the school debate team and was at a practice session, but she expected to see Gillian and Nia. She was surprised not to find them at home. Before she left for the day, Mrs. Lucia informed her that although the Stewart's housekeeper hadn't called to inform the household of a delay, she was sure that she would be along shortly. Reassured, Nedra hadn't started worrying until nearly an hour passed and the girls still weren't home.

She called Mrs. Sharon's cell phone and the Stewart landline, but got voice mail both times. When Mrs. Sharon returned her call a short while ago and asked how the girls liked the limousine ride home that was when Nedra became concerned.

After listening to the housekeeper recount the telephone call that she received from Thad, Nedra disconnected and was about to dial Darnell's cell phone when she spotted Sin's car coming up the driveway. While she was watching him pull into the garage, Nedra's phone rang. It was Darnell.

Thad Stewart noted the excitement on his wife's face as he drove along the highway. Each mile was taking them closer to home and closer to Nia. They had missed her terribly. After their little girl started school, Darnell and Thad arranged their schedules to make sure that one of them was at home whenever the other one was away on business. Unfortunately, necessity had taken them both away from her this time.

They had paid the price for that decision with loneliness and longing for their only child. Thad was as excited about going home as his wife. He couldn't wait to hear Nia squeal Daddy when she saw him. To him, that one word was worth everything in the world.

"We're getting close so I'm calling her now," Darnell told him as she withdrew her cell phone.

Thad and she would often play a little game with their daughter if either one was away on a trip. They would call and describe how close they were to her until they arrived at the front door and then yell, "I'm here!" They would then smother her with hugs and kisses. Darnell could hardly wait.

She was just about to hit speed dial when Dana's call to her delayed her own.

"Well, hello!" Darnell greeted her aunt cheerfully.

"Where are you?" Dana asked. The levity with which she was greeted was not returned.

Darnell caught the sober tone. Her smile faded.

"Thad and I are coming in from the airport. We're on the highway not far from home. Why? What's wrong?"

The last two words caught Thad's attention. He glanced at his wife.

On the other end, Dana sat behind her desk wanting more than anything for this to be a nightmare from which she could awaken. Glancing briefly at James Starr, who was sitting sat across from her, she gave a shaky sigh.

"Ask Thad to pull over. I've got something to tell you both."

Darnell's heart lurched. Whatever was wrong was serious. Relaying her aunt's message to Thad, she watched him take the exit that would lead to their house and pull to the side of the road. He gave Darnell a fear filled glance. His wife put her cell phone on speaker.

Dana could think of no way to soften the blow. "Nia and Gillian have been kidnapped."

Shaken, neither Thad nor Darnell wasted any time asking questions. Darnell disconnected the call and hit speed dial. Nedra answered.

"Is Nia there?" Darnell demanded simultaneously.

"No she's not." Nedra couldn't mask the tremor of fear in her voice. She told them what Mrs. Sharon had said about a limo picking the girls up.

Darnell gave a strangled gasp. Thad's expletive was explosive before he confirmed the worst.

"I didn't call anybody!"

Sin could hear Thad's booming voice coming from his wife's cell phone when he walked into the living room. One look at his wife's tear stained face had him hurrying to her.

"What's going on?"

"It's the girls." That was all that Nedra could manage to say. She handed him the telephone and walked away. She placed her hands on her mouth to stifle the scream that threatened to erupt from the depths of her soul.

Sin was unprepared for what his brother-in-law had to say. The words were like an arrow piercing his heart.

"We're ten minutes away from your house," Thad told him as he skidded back onto the highway. "Call Dana."

****

Dana suspected that Thad broke speed records getting to the Reasoner house. She and the couple had been on FaceTime less than five minutes when Darnell and Thad burst into the family room.

Both couples looked shell shocked as Dana recounted the message that the distorted male voice had relayed. She also told them about the package that had been delivered to her office.

"What's in it?" Sin asked grimly.

Dana swallowed the lump in her throat. "Nia's pink purse."

Without thinking, she reached for the opened box to show it to them. James grabbed her wrist, halting her action. Their eyes met. He had taken his sunglasses off and Dana had been startled by the color of his eyes. They were light gray. As she looked into them they sent a silent reminder not to touch the contents with her hands.

Dana's hesitation in producing the package alerted the others that she was not alone. James had been sitting to the side, out of sight.

Sin tensed. "Who's there with you?"

James moved in front of the screen. "My name is James Starr."

Sin blinked. James remained stoic. Dana and the others were too preoccupied to notice the flicker of recognition between the two men. Dana explained how James found the package.

"And why is he still there?" Sin wanted to know.

Dana wasn't sure how to answer that. She said the first thing that came to her mind.

"He's an ex-cop. His expertise might be useful."

"A cop? Thad shrilled. "What the hell, Dana! You said that the caller warned you not to get the police involved!"

James understood the man's apprehension. "As she said, I'm an *ex*-cop, but I have advised her to contact the FBI."

His words brought instant reactions from both couples. There was a chorus of competing voices as everyone gave their opinion, both for and against that suggestion. Sin remained silent as he continued to stare daggers at the man who had appeared beside Dana so unexpectedly.

"How do we know that you're not involved?"

Sin's words halted all conversation. Everyone's attention turned back to the man on the screen. James looked at him steadily.

"The authorities will rule that out when they get here. As for now, the longer we wait to contact them the more danger those girls are in."

Sin's jaws tightened. Despite his feelings toward the man sitting at Dana's side, he could not dispute what he was saying. He turned toward the others.

"It is urgent that we get to our girls quickly."

Giving James another hostile glare, he went to Nedra. Taking her cold hands into his, he looked into her eyes. He wasn't coy.

"Chances are whoever took the girls wanted Nia."

Nedra needed no further explanation. She knew instantly what he meant. Gillian might be expendable.

.Nedra was optimistic. "But they had to know that the girls are related. They must know that they could increase the ransom by having both of them."

Thad agreed. He addressed Dana.

"On our way over here I called Mrs. Sharon and asked her about the person who called about the limo. She said that it was a man who sounded exactly like me. She hadn't recognized the telephone number when she answered the phone, but she didn't think anything of it because we could have been anywhere when the call was made. That's happened before. Whoever it was did their homework. They knew at least one of our landline numbers. They knew that we were out of town, and that Mrs. Sharon was to pick the girls up. They must have been watching us to know our schedules. If they knew all of this about us they must know that the girls are cousins."

"They had to be watching you too, Dana," Sin added, "because they knew that you were in your office. Were you alone when he called?"

"Yes, I was."

"Someone must be familiar with the office personnel and watched them leave." James offered in explanation.

"And then you showed up." Sin made no attempt to conceal his antagonism or his suspicion. This time everyone noticed.

"I *showed up* and told her to call the FBI," James reminded him, "just like I'm advising the rest of you to do."

Ignoring his comment, Sin addressed Dana. "Did the caller say when he would call back?"

"No, but that was over an hour ago and…"

The ring of Dana's cell phone interrupted her in midsentence. She had placed it on top of her desk. She checked caller ID and didn't recognize the number.

"It's nobody I know.

"Then answer it." Sin's words were not a request but a demand. .

In tune with what Sin was thinking, James picked up the cell phone and handed it to Dana. "Answer it."

Despite the hostility emanating between Sin and James, it was obvious that at the moment they were in perfect sync. Dana did as directed.

"Hello?"

"Two million dollars in 24 hours," were the chilling words that greeted her.

Dana's hand began to tremble. Turning to the others she silently mouthed the words, "It's him."

CHAPTER 4

"He has my cell phone number!" Dana told the investigator with whom she was speaking. "How in the hell did he get my freakin' cell phone number?" She was furious.

James and she were in the conference room in her office, where the two of them were being interrogated by the FBI.

After the second call from the kidnappers there was a consensus that the authorities should be contacted. The FBI had responded with amazing speed and efficiency. By nightfall they inconspicuously set up operations both in L.A. and on the Peninsula. Dressed as gardeners, yardmen, janitors and city utility workers, they blended seamlessly into the areas that they infiltrated.

Telephone lines were tapped, waiting to trace the next call that Dana might receive. The instructions that she had been given by the abductors were simple and precise. She was to deliver the money tomorrow. The drop off point was on the Santa Monica pier, an area which was especially crowded on weekends.

After the instructions were given, Dana made a request to speak with the girls, but it was ignored. The abductors made certain that their communication with her was brief. That avoided a trace being put on the call. Adding to everyone's stress, the families were told that after the money was delivered the girls would not be released together. One would be released after the money was retrieved. The other one would be released after it was counted and it was confirmed that no tracking device had been included. Both releases were to be somewhere on the Peninsula.

Everyone was shaken by the telephone calls, and before the authorities arrived, each family member got busy. Sin and Thad made arrangements to get the ransom money. Nedra contacted two sons at their respective schools to make sure that they were safe. She arranged for them to come home. Darnell called Mrs. Sharon and asked her to come to the Reasoner home. She could provide valuable information to the authorities about the telephone call that Thad was suppose to have made.

Dana noticed with pride that despite the dreadful circumstances, nobody in her family was falling apart and she was determined that she wouldn't either. Most of her life she had felt as though she was the weak link in her extraordinary family. She had spent the past two years in the bosom of those who loved her as she recovered from a fall that she suffered in her home. It was during that time of recovery that she discovered how wrong she had been about herself. She *was* a strong woman, and she had learned to appreciate her strengths.

This present ordeal demanded that she utilize every ounce of that strength. If her niece, nephew and cousins could endure this nightmare and stay sane, so could she. Of course they had each other to lean on for support and she had no one. So, she was grateful that James Starr had inadvertently stumbled into this nightmare. He was proving to be a godsend.

When the abductor was making his demands, using quick thinking, James hit the speaker on her cell phone and withdrew a tiny recorder from the pocket of his jeans and recorded the abductor's voice. Dana wanted to drop on her knees with gratitude for his having done that. Even

Sinclair, who was openly hostile toward James, seemed appreciative. Yet, Agent Michael Conway, the FBI's lead investigator on this case, seemed to think that James having a recorder was suspect.

"You say that you carry it around with you to take notes on your cases?" His tone was skeptical.

Dana wasn't sure what to think about the agent's manner. She didn't really know anything about James, but her gut instincts told her that he wasn't involved with the abductors. Did the authorities know something that she didn't know?

James seemed to take the inquiries in stride. He didn't get upset. None of the many questions that the authorities asked seemed to faze him. He answered them all politely and appeared ready to cooperate in any way that he could. She had to admit that James Starr was a cool customer.

Before the authorities arrived, Dana tried to get his take on the abductors' actions and to find out a little about James.

"From the way this abduction was set up, with the money drop being in L.A. but the kids being released on the Peninsula, I think that there are at least two kidnappers," she speculated. "What do you think?"

James agreed. "I'm no kidnapping expert, but as far as I know most ransom deliveries and releases are in the same area.

They both understood that the dual operation might make it more difficult to capture the culprits. The idea that the criminals might get away with this was unthinkable as far as Dana was concerned.

"How long have you been in the security business, Mr. Starr?" she asked coyly.

James smiled to himself at the sudden change in direction. She was fishing for information.

"First of all, please call me James, and to answer your question I've been in this business for five years. My partner is a private investigator and we merged our businesses two years ago. I moved out here to establish a West Coast branch in Southern California."

"Who's your partner?"

"His name is Nathan Webb. Ray knows him. Nate has twenty-five years of experience as a P.I."

Dana's interest piqued. "And what do your services include?"

"Webb Starr offers everything from assessing the security of commercial and residential property to following a straying husband or wife."

Dana raised a brow. "Oh really? How many employees do you have?"

"Presently, we have twenty-five in two states, and as I said earlier, we're ready to open an office in Northern California. Speaking of that, I need to call my partner and let him know that I've had a slight delay in getting up there." He withdrew his cell phone from his pocket.

"Don't worry, I won't tell him the reason why," he added in reaction to her censuring glare.

James was on the telephone talking to his partner when the FBI arrived. By the time the authorities came, Dana was feeling much more secure about James Starr since she knew a little more about him. However, as Agent Conway continued to focus on him, she wasn't quite sure that she had learned enough.

"We've run your name through our computer. Mr. Starr," the agent told him ominously, "and I'm sure that you can guess what we've discovered."

James' casual stance didn't waver. "What was that?"

Yes, what was it? Dana was on full alert.

The agent gave him a twisted smile. "It seems that you've had quite a colorful past."

Dana raised a brow. *A colorful past?*

James didn't react to that observation either. "It has been interesting."

"Indeed, but as you're undoubtedly aware, we have to look at all aspects of this case and consider every possibility. We've dug deep considering how little time we've had."

"Then let me commend you." James gave a sardonic smile. He knew that the agent was baiting him, but he beat him to the punch. "I take it that you're referring to my activities as a hot headed youth."

The agent nodded. "I am."

Dana frowned. "What youthful activities? What does that mean? I hope that there are no secrets here."

James could see that she was impatient. He didn't make her wait.

"You see, Mrs. Mansfield, what the agent is trying not to say is that it seems coincidental that I should stumble into this situation given my background…"

"What background? Would you please get to the point?"

"Okay. Despite my fifteen years as a cop with a clean record or my five years in the security field, I still can't escape the fact that in my youth I was involved with one of the most notorious gangs in Harlem, New York. I'm a former gang member."

Dana didn't bat an eyelash at that revelation. Looking at him, she wasn't surprised.

****

Gillian Reasoner was smart. By the time that she entered kindergarten her older brothers had taught her to read on a second grade level. Just as important, Gillian was also a clever child. She possessed a blend of quick thinking and basic common sense which belied a child her age. Grownups often marveled at her ability to finesse her way out of trouble, which she found herself in much too often. That was because Gillian Reasoner was also tough.

Born to a drug addicted teenage mother, she barely weighed three pounds at birth. She was a child who had to fight for her life from the beginning. The little girl with the dimpled chin and sad eyes was three years old when she became the daughter of Nedra and Sinclair Reasoner. As the youngest of the Reasoner's three adopted children, she held a special place in her family's heart. They adored her, and allowed her energetic personality to thrive. The diminutive cutie was dubbed Little Miss Dynamite by her family. Being held against her will by anyone presented the perfect opportunity for that keg of dynamite to explode.

It hadn't taken Gillian long to figure out that she was extra baggage for the kidnappers. It was obvious that the room in which they were being held captives had been set up for one person. If these people were smart they would ask for money from both set of parents, doubling their take. If they weren't smart she didn't want to think about what her fate might be. Whatever the case, Nia and she were both in danger as long as they were here. They needed to escape.

Gillian had developed a plan. By looking through the doggy door she could see a bathroom across the hall with a window. She would ask the kidnappers if Nia and she could go to the facilities together. If the men let them out, the girls would close the bathroom door and run the water to cover the noise while they opened the window. Nia would climb out first and Gillian would follow. Gillian had instructed her cousin to run and keep running whether Gillian got out with her or not.

Time passed slowly as they waited in the hot, stuffy room for the kidnapper to come to the door. The heat was stifling. The air vent above them didn't seem to be working well. Gillian took the plastic off of the mattress and pillow because laying on it was too hot. She also turned the light off at intervals because it added to the heat.

Not knowing if it was day or night, Gillian looked out of the doggy door across the hall to see if there was still daylight streaming through the window into the bathroom. It was dark. She wasn't sure how long it had been since they were kidnapped, but they both wanted to go home.

****

As he settled into his airplane seat the stranger gave a sigh of relief. It had been quite a trek to get here from the island on which he resided. He made the airline reservation the day that he read the two year old article about Darnell Cameron. It hadn't taken him long to pack and close his house, but the boat ride to the mainland had been grueling. The flight in a small plane to the coast was just as laborious. From there he caught a jet to the United States. He sorely missed the private aircraft that once took him to any destination that he desired, and the luxury yacht on which he used to cruise the ports of the world. Things had certainly changed, but the sacrifices were worth it because he was still alive. He couldn't complain.

Having made this unexpected return to the States, he couldn't help but ask himself how long he would stay alive if someone from his past spotted him. What he was doing could possibly seal his fate. He was taking a risk making this trip, but the first hurdle had been crossed. The fake passport that he hoped he would never have to use again had gotten him through customs. He was onboard the plane now where he could lay back, get some rest and wake up in Los Angeles. The question was what would he do when he got there? He had no plan.

His decision to come here had been so spur of the moment that he hadn't thought about that little detail. What he had read had been so startling, so unexpected, so shocking, that all he could think about at the time was getting to the States, and quickly. There was no way that he could have stayed on the island not knowing if what he read was true. As far as he was concerned, if it cost him his life to know the truth, it would be worth it.

CHAPTER 5

"We'll get a decoy to make the drop," Agent Conway informed Dana as they reviewed plans for the delivery of the ransom. After a long session of strategic planning, the FBI made arrangements for a bank to deliver the money requested by the abductors, making certain that each bill was carefully marked to avoid detection.

James sat quietly, observing everything happening around him. He knew that the authorities still held him suspect, but he wasn't concerned. He had been vetted years ago when he joined the NYPD. His youthful indiscretions were well documented—at least those that he wanted others to know about.

The revelation of his past didn't appear to bother Dana Mansfield. The look that she gave him after hearing the facts indicated that she thought what was revealed might have been worse. She had no idea that was probably true.

Dana asked him to stay until after the drop was made, stating that she might need his expertise. He had no doubt that the request was actually made out of fear that he might go to the media with the story of the abduction. She wanted to keep an eye on him. James was certain that if she hadn't insisted that he stay, Agent Conway would have. Either way, the lives of two children were at stake and although it delayed his personal plans, James had no problem being here.

This case was big, and every agent scurrying around Dana's office knew it. Darnell Cameron and Thad Stewart were two of the biggest stars in the world. When the story eventually broke, every aspect of the abduction was going to be scrutinized by the media and by the public. The FBI was treading carefully. The end result had better be successful, or heads would roll.

Dana and the parents of the girls were being handled with kid gloves. Each family member was questioned regarding their activities during the day, with James and Mrs. Sharon, being outside the family, receiving the most intense scrutiny

The Stewart's housekeeper was put under particular pressure since it was she who spoke to the man claiming to be Thad Stewart. Her interrogation was so intense, and upset the older woman to such an extent, that Conway received a message from Darnell Cameron Stewart informing him that she did not appreciate the way that her housekeeper was being treated.

After that, the contact between the L.A. and the Carmel operations became more discrete, and James was unable to gauge how the Stewarts and the Reasoners were holding up. However, he did notice that Dana seemed to be more focused than she was when they first encountered each other.

Between breaks in the FBI questioning, he and Dana had the opportunity to talk. Haunted by the fact that the kidnapper contacted her on her cell phone, James helped her make a list of how many people had the number. By the time she was finished writing names down, she had to admit that her cell phone number wasn't as private as she thought.

In observing the seemingly endless activity swirling around her, Dana was proud of herself for her ability to look calm. The reality was that her insides felt like jell-o and she prayed silently, and constantly, for the safe return of the young girls. As time passed, she began to feel more confident that the girls could be returned safely. The efficiency with which the authorities operated was impressive. She was glad that the family had listened to James.

His advice was sound and unhampered by the emotions clouding the judgment of the girls' loved ones. His objectivity was needed.

Dana liked James Starr. She liked his laid back style, his calm demeanor. It was comforting. His presence made her feel safe. There was no doubt that his towering height and muscled build was an important factor. He had the physique of a man who had spent time behind bars. She hadn't been surprised when it was revealed that in the past he'd had run-ins with the law. He claimed to be a different man now, and she had no reason to doubt him.

Yet, Dana had to admit that his gray-eyed gaze was disconcerting. They seemed to change with his emotions, and she noticed that they missed very little. He was keenly observant, and she had the feeling that if the FBI missed anything in this case, he would notice, and *that* was exactly what was needed.

****

Gillian fought to stay awake in the suffocating heat. Both girls were dehydrated and Nia had fallen asleep. Each time Gillian felt herself drifting off she jerked awake, but as the seconds ticked away it was becoming more and more difficult.

She was fighting the overpowering urge to sleep when she heard the faintest of sounds outside the door. Alerted, she sat up and listened closely. Someone was there. It was time to execute her plan for escape.

"Hello!" Gillian cried loudly. She turned the light on and crawled off of the mattress toward the door. "Is somebody out there? We need to use the bathroom."

On the other side of the door her words were met with silence.

"There's no place for us to go in here!"

Silence.

"Can you take us to the bathroom? We really have to go bad!"

Silence.

"It's hot in here and we're about to burst!"

Once again there was silence. It lasted so long that she decided that her plea had been ignored. She returned to the mattress. Nia was waking up, when suddenly there was movement at the doggie door. Gillian turned in time to see the bottom of a small, metal pail being maneuvered through the opening. It landed on the tile floor.

Gillian retrieved it and peeked inside. She found two baloney sandwiches and two bottles of water, along with a single roll of wrapped toilet paper. Her heart sank as she realized that her plan would not be put into action. Neither of them would be leaving this room to use the bathroom.

Tossing the food and water aside, she threw the toilet paper at the wall as hard as she could. The cover on the roll burst as the roll landed on the floor with a soft thud. But, her rage still wasn't appeased. Taking the bucket by the handle, Gillian beat the pail against the wall again and again until the metal handle came off in her hand. Spent, she let the battered pail fall to the floor, its practical purpose now in doubt.

Gillian fought to contain her tears as she joined Nia on the mattress. The little girl light brown eyes were wide with shock at having witnessed her cousin's display of temper.

"Are we going to the bathroom?" She asked timidly.

Gillian indicated the misshapen pail lying on the floor. "We'll have to use that."

Nia looked at the pail. Her face registered confusion.

"That's not a toilet. Aren't we going over to the bathroom?"

"They're not going to let us," Gillian told her honestly. Her heart felt heavy with every word. She wasn't sure if that window across the hallway was too high for them to jump to the ground or just right for such an escape. All she knew was that it was a way out. It might be their only hope for freedom.

"So we can't go home?" Nia's chin began to quiver. She tried to hold back the tears.

Gillian didn't answer. She gave her cousin a hug, opened a bottle of cold water and bathed the girl's hot face with its coolness, before planting a comforting kiss on her brow. With one last act of resentment she threw the bucket handle across the room. It settled beneath the doggy door.

Urging Nia from the mattress, she placed her over the pail to relieve herself. Both girls had stripped to their underwear because of the oppressive heat.

"I don't like this," Nia balked, but she relieved herself anyway, and Gillian followed suit.

"It smells like pee in here," Nia griped as the girls wiped their hands with toilet paper and settled back on the mattress.

"We'll put the bucket back outside," Gillian told her.

She knew that would only be a temporary solution. Matters would be worse when they both relieved themselves of solid waste. Gillian refused to settle for this! There had to be a way out of here.

Looking around the bare room, her eyes shifted to the metal handle lying on the floor. It had been attached to the pail with screws that were now scattered about the room. Suddenly an idea came to her.

Hurrying to the door, Gillian listened carefully for any sounds coming from the other side. Not hearing any, she grabbed the curved metal handle and, once again, stuck her head through the doggy door. She tried to put an arm through at the same time, but was unsuccessful. After trying several maneuvers, she was able to position herself so that she could put her arm through the door and extend it as far as she could. It could reach where the door knob used to be, but her goal was to reach beyond that with the handle in her hand. If she was successful, then she might be able to reach the slide latch that kept them prisoners in this room. All she needed was something to put through the hole in the bucket handle where the screws used to be. She would then make a device that might be able to catch the latch and open the door. It was a long shot, but it was a chance worth taking.

Shimmying back into the room, the fear and anger that gripped her minutes ago was replaced by the fire of defiance. The guile that Gillian had honed over the years was about to be put to the test. If her plan worked she and Nia would be out of their hated prison soon.

CHAPTER 6

Darnell called her mother, Bev, who was Dana's older sister. Bev and her husband, Ray, hurried to the Reasoner home. On their arrival at the house, Ray was both surprised and happy to see James Starr in Dana's office, and he assured the authorities and the family that Ray was not suspect. Dana was already convinced of that. She and James took advantage of any breaks during the day to get acquainted.

While activity swirled around them, the two of them settled on the sofa in Dana's office, sipping endless cups of coffee and feasting on the carryout food brought in by the agents. James entertained her with stories about his years on the force. Some of the antidotes were funny, others were tragic, but Dana noticed that he was guarded when it came to revealing personal information.

He did share that he wasn't married, and he told her about his reputation as a rebel when he was a police officer. Having been on the other side of the law when he was young, he confessed to having had more empathy with the bad guys than he should have.

After he finished his storytelling James asked Dana about her years as an attorney. Her stories weren't as exciting as his. Respecting the personal lives of her celebrity clients, she didn't gossip about them. Instead, she told him about their devotion to their families, their consideration for others and about their charitable efforts, which were often anonymous. After she finished, James looked at her approvingly.

"I like your discretion. I hope your clients appreciate it."

"They do." Dana was pleased by the compliment.

"But, there's something else I want to know."

Dana looked at him warily. She didn't plan on revealing anything else, so what more could he want? The answer surprised her.

"Tell me something about Gillian and Nia. What kind of girls are they? What are their personalities like?"

It was then that Dana realized that he was the only one during this whole ordeal who had asked that question. The agents wanted to know the girls' physical descriptions and what they were wearing when they were snatched. No one asked about *them*. What was even more impressive was that he really seemed to care about the answer.

As Dana told him about the girls, she noticed how attentively he listened, and she appreciated the distraction he was providing. For the first time since the abductor's contacted her, Dana found herself dwelling on the positive.

"Little Nia is a beautiful child. She's got her mother's large, expressive eyes and her father's dimpled cheeks, but she's more than a pretty face. She's smart and has the sweetest personality, although she's a little bit shy until she gets to know you. She's gentle and kind and very feminine. She loves dressing up."

"What about her cousin?"

Dana chuckled as she visualized Gillian Reasoner. "Now there's a character! The stories that I can tell you about her you wouldn't believe. She's the boldest, most determined child I have ever met. She's a little thing, really small for her age, but she's a born leader. If I had two words to describe her best those words would be pit bull."

James laughed at the description. "I like them both already."

"It takes their parents to really tell you about them. Both of the girls are the lights of their lives."

"No doubt," James remembered a time when he experienced the same feeling about someone.

As she thought about the girls, Dana was pleased that she could find levity at a time like this. "I'll tell you one thing, wherever they are you can bet your life that Gillian's scheming to find a way home."

****

Before embarking on their quest to escape their imprisonment, Gillian and Nia said a prayer asking God to help them. Gillian's mother had told her that people don't always get what they ask for when they ask for it, but God did his best. She was hoping that this would be the case today.

She and Nia worked together to orchestrate their escape. Before going to school this morning, Gillian tied a colorful satin ribbon around Nia's Afro puff when she fashioned her cousin's hair style. They used that hair ribbon to help make the lasso that would catch the latch on the lock. Little had she realized when she added the ribbon to Nia's hair how useful it would become.

She managed to thread the thin piece of satin through the empty screw hole in the handle of the pail. Having done that, she then repositioned herself at the doggy door at just the right angle so that she could use her arm to loop the makeshift lasso onto the knob on the latch. Each attempt was made blindly, but despite this, the young girl hoped that her efforts would be successful. If the loop hit its target, a couple of tugs should release the latch and offer them freedom.

She tried countless times and missed, but she kept on trying, remaining constantly aware of any sound that would alert her that her captors were approaching. When her arm grew numb, and she became dizzy from the heat and the effort, she gave Nia instructions on how to proceed, and the five year old took Gillian's place at the doggy door. Unfortunately, her arm was too short to offer much chance of success, but while Gillian rested Nia was tireless in her effort.

Gillian was so proud of her little cousin. The blistering heat, the smell of their own urine, and the Spartan conditions in which they were forced to stay was taking its toll on them both, but Nia proved to be a fighter. There were some tears, but no whining. She did whatever Gillian requested with no complaint.

When her arm felt better, she sent Nia back to the mattress to rest. Gillian was exhausted and wanted to sleep, but she knew that she had to keep trying. Their lives might depend on it.

Time passed and she worked tirelessly. Nia took cat naps, waking occasionally to ask the same question.

"Are we going home yet?" It was the hope in the little girl's eyes that kept Gillian going.

Drained by the heat, Nia jerked awake, and wiped the sweat from her eyes. Looking across the room she could see Gillian's lower body bathed in the light from the goose neck lamp as she continuously tossed the noose toward the latch.

Perspiration poured from them both. The heat was sapping all of their strength. Sitting up sleepily, this time

Nia directed a different question to Gillian.

"Do you want me to pray to God again for help?"

Scooting back into the room, Gillian's face was drenched with tears of frustration mixed with the sweat of exertion. Wiping the moisture from her face, she leaned against the door and massaged her sore arm. Earlier she assured Nia that their prayers were going straight to heaven.

"And you know that my mother says that our prayers are really powerful, and she should know since she's a minister."

This time she answered Nia's question with, "It couldn't hurt."

Taking a sip from the water bottle, she watched as Nia slid onto her knees and began to pray. She was so weak from the heat that she swayed, but she stayed on her knees.

"Our Father, who is in heaven…"

Gillian resumed her position in the doggy door. Her strength was waning, but not her will. She lost count of the number of times that she tossed the noose upward, but she was prepared to repeat the action until she dropped. Once again she waited for the slack that would mean that her efforts had failed again, but there was no slack on the line this time. Gillian stilled.

"Thy kingdom come…"

She pulled on the pail handle lightly, no give.

"Thy will be done…"

The ribbon had hooked onto something.

"On earth…"

Gillian gave the handle a tug, but in her direction this time.

"As it is in heaven"

Gillian tugged harder.

"Give us this day..."

There was a click. Nia froze. Her eyes slid toward her cousin.

Gillian slid from the doggy door back into the room. She was afraid to breathe. Gillian's eyes met her cousin's eyes. They both turned their attention to the wooden door.

Since there was no handle, Gillian pulled the bottom of the doggy door. The wood door opened a crack. Air rushed into the room. To the girls it felt like an Arctic blast.

They looked at each other and grinned. God had done his very best for them on this day.

Moving quickly, Gillian knew there was no time to waste. Their captors might make an appearance at any moment.

With renewed energy the girls quickly bundled their clothing and shoes, not bothering to squander their time dressing. Gillian grabbed a bottle of water and turned the light off in the room. Listening carefully for any sound, they eased the creaking wooden door open carefully and squeezed through it. The waft of air that greeted them when they stepped into the dark hallway was welcomed, but they didn't have time to enjoy it. Closing the door behind them, Gillian locked it back firmly and removed the incriminating lasso from the latch, taking it with her.

Scurrying to the bathroom, the girls closed the door behind them hoping to muffle any sounds that might be made when they opened the window. As they approached it, Gillian whispered a prayer that they weren't being held in an apartment building twenty stories high.

For the second time that day her prayer was answered. The latch on the window proved simple to unlock. The drop to the ground wasn't far. Gillian helped Nia outside first, with instructions to run if she told her to do so. Handing her their bundles, Gillian stole back to the bathroom door and then cracked it open as it had been when they entered the room. Hurriedly, she climbed out of the window, taking the pains to close it behind her, leaving no clue that she and Nia were no longer confined. Taking her bundle from her cousin, she took her by the hand and in the muted light of an early morning sunrise, the two small figures raced from the house like gazelles in flight.

CHAPTER 7

When Saturday morning dawned in L.A., everyone was exhausted. No one caught more than catnaps all night. Most of the evening was spent reviewing every possible person that Dana knew who could be a suspect in this case. She went through her files thoroughly trying to come up with the name of anyone she knew who might have committed this appalling act.

She was an entertainment attorney and her clients were wealthy members of the entertainment industry. As far as she knew no one of her acquaintance was so financially strapped that they would commit a federal crime.

It was Agent Conway's suggestion that she consider those people she knew who might be jealous of the Stewart's enormous success. She thought the question naïve.

"Are you kidding?" Dana scoffed. "This is Hollywood. Everybody is jealous of everybody."

However James suggested other avenues. "I'm sure you guys are checking out the building staff: the janitors, the security staff, and etcetera. They usually have master keys that admit them to all of the offices in a building. That would give them access to a lot of information."

Agent Conway bristled at the suggestion. "We're doing that." He seemed peeved that James might be trying to upstage him.

Taking it in stride, James quipped to Dana, "I seem to piss the cops off on all levels."

48

****

An exhausted Sinclair Reasoner leaned against the center isle in his dressing room with his cell phone pressed to his ear. Not wanting Nedra to hear his conversation, he had closed the door.

His efforts to get his wife to rest were unsuccessful. Neither of them had slept all night. They couldn't sleep as long as their daughter wasn't home. A few hours ago the rising sun had announced the arrival of a new day. Only adrenaline kept them all going. But, he wasn't concerned about himself. He was worried about Nedra—but help was on the way.

"We just landed," Marva Davis told her son-in-law, referring to the private plane that had been sent for her. "It was a smooth ride all of the way."

"Good." Sin breathed a sigh of relief. "There's an agent waiting for you at the gate. We don't know who might be watching, so he's dressed like a limo driver."

"All right. How's everyone doing?" The concern in his mother-in-law's voice mirrored his own.

"We're holding up." Sin pinched the bridge of his nose. He was so tired that his eyes were aching. "Darnell and Thad are staying here with us. Bev and Ray are holding the fort down at their house. Colin drove home from Stanford. We wanted to make sure that he was safe. Both of the boys seem to be hanging in there."

"How about you? How are you doing?"

For the first time since this nightmare began Sin managed a smile. How he loved this woman. She was not only his mother-in-law, but his friend, his buddy. When he married her daughter, Marva had been an extra bonus. He had a seven room "cottage" built for her on their property for her to use whenever she came to visit. It was his hope that when his mother-in-law decided to retire as the minister of the church that she led in Kansas City, Missouri, she would make the cottage her home.

"I'm doing okay," Sin replied without much conviction.

"No you're not," Marva said softly. "You're hurting, and it's okay for you to feel the pain. Just remember that I love you and that you're in my prayers."

"Thanks, Marva," It was taking everything for him to contain his emotions.

He was glad that he contacted Marva. After speaking to her, he felt better.   Nedra hadn't wanted her to know what had happened. She didn't want to alarm her. Sin disagreed and defied his wife's wishes. Darnell had her mother there to comfort her. He figured that his wife needed her mother there for her as well.

Sin had withdrawn from the others, needing to find a quiet place where he could be alone. After wandering their property for a while, eventually he drifted upstairs still trying to reconcile the mix of emotions consuming him. Fear gripped the very core of his being as he thought about what could happen to his daughter and his niece. Yet, it was the rage at the audacity of the act that he kept trying to keep at bay. That was proving difficult.

There was a knock on his closet door. He knew it was Nedra. Tucking his cell phone in his pocket, he called out.

"Come in."

She entered and quickly closed the distance between them as she walked into his arms and placed her head on his chest. They tightened their arms around one another, each acting as an anchor for the other. Through the tears they shed together, they vowed that they would survive this, and so would Gillian and Nia.

It was a little over two years ago that Sin discovered that he had a sister. Prior to that Nedra and their children was the only family that he had. His drug addicted mother died when he was ten years old. At the time, he had no idea who his father was. He had been alone in the world.

Sin grew up a child of the streets, hustling and breaking the law at a whim, going in and out of juvenile detention. He respected no one. He cared about no one. He wore the label "bad boy" with pride.

As an adult, he turned his life completely around, but love was an elusive part of his existence until he met Reverend Nedra Davis. She changed his whole world, crawling into places inside his heart that he wasn't aware existed. She made him believe in possibilities that he never considered. He worshipped his wife and adored their three children.

Gillian was their baby, their precocious, pugnacious little girl. Anybody who knew her knew that nobody messed with Gillian or with her loved ones. If they did, they would suffer the consequences. The child was fearless.

Earlier, in an attempt to relieve some of the tension in the household, Trevor Reasoner had quipped, "I almost feel sorry for Gillian's kidnappers."

Everyone in the family laughed. They knew exactly what he meant. Gillian Reasoner could prove to be a handful when she wanted to be. There was little doubt that she was giving her abductors hell.

"I'm glad Nia is with her," Darnell told the family. "Maybe then my baby won't be so scared."

Sin hugged his sister to him, just as he was doing with his wife. He told Darnell the same thing he kept telling Nedra.

"Everything is going to be all right."

It seemed as though the family was saying those words to each other a lot since this ordeal began. Faith and prayer were the only things that sustained them. Even Sin whispered a tentative word to a Higher Power that he wasn't sure existed—but, just in case.

"Do you still think that James Starr might be involved in all of this?" Nedra asked. Still encircled in the comfort of her husband's arms she felt him tense at the mention of Starr's name.

Sin hesitated. "I'm not sure. I guess it's possible that he did stumble into this whole thing by accident."

Sin had told Nedra as well as relayed to the FBI his familiarity with James Starr. Although it came as no surprise to Sin that the authorities ran James Starr's name through their system, it did surprise him when it was verified that Starr's claim to being an ex-cop was true. Nevertheless, while that fact might have given James Starr a pass as far as the authorities were concerned, it didn't impress Sin. The gulf between the two men was too great; the antagonism on Sin's part was too profound. He hated the man!

A loud knock on the bedroom door drew their attention. It was followed by Trevor's inquiry.

"Mama? Dad? Are you in there?"

It was time to return to the nightmare. The couple headed to the door.

"We're coming," Sin informed their son.

"Grandma's here. She just pulled up."

Closing the door behind him, they could hear his sneakered footsteps hurrying down the hall. Nedra perked up. In spite of the fact that her husband had called her mother against her wishes she knew the decision had been the right one. Her presence was sorely needed. Marva Davis was a powerful force in all of their lives.

"I have to call Brandon and thank him for sending his plane for her," Sin told his wife.

Nedra could hear the regret in her husband's voice. He had called his best friend and asked for the favor without an explanation. Brandon complied without question, although Sin knew that the veteran reporter and media mogul sensed that something was out of the ordinary.

She knew that Sin had wanted to share what was happening with his friend. He needed his support and comfort, especially since Brandon and his wife, Sash, had been through the same nightmare with their son years ago.

Nedra was equally as sorry that she couldn't tell her best friend, Carla Ryan-Belle, what was happening. They were as close as sisters. Gillian was her godchild; but for security purposes, the FBI had forbidden the parents from sharing information about the abduction with anyone other than close family members. Reluctantly, everyone abided by the request.

Downstairs the household was abuzz with activity. The agents assigned to the Reasoner home were busy going about their business. Bev and Ray had arrived at the house in time to welcome Marva. Mrs. Sharon was there as well.

The authorities wouldn't allow her to go home to her family until the situation was resolved. Since the Reasoner housekeeper had left before becoming aware of the abduction, the Stewart's housekeeper volunteered to cook breakfast for the assortment of guests, including the agents. As they dined, the family updated Marva on the latest developments.

After listening, she suggested a group prayer. Holding hands, the family formed a circle and with heads bowed waited for Marva to speak. Sin's cell phone rang, interrupting the gathering. Nedra gave him a disapproving look. Reaching into his pocket he turned the instrument off, allowing Marva to proceed.

"Lord, you know why we're here, and I'm going to make this short and simple. You are in charge of everything great and small. This is in your hands. Please bring our babies home."

There was a chorus of amens as everyone hugged, passing on the strength that they needed to get through this crisis. Sin stepped aside and checked the number of his last caller. The world might be in turmoil inside his home, but it continued to revolve outside of it.

The area code was not in their area. He didn't recognize the number, dismissed it as unimportant and was about to pocket the cell phone again when it vibrated and the same number appeared. This time, he answered it. The voice on the other end caused his knees to buckle.

"Daddy! It's me! I need you to come and get me and Nia. Now!"

****

"Welcome to our establishment, Mr…" the desk clerk glanced down at the name on the registration card. "Mr. Hardman. We hope you enjoy our city."

The stranger acknowledged her greeting with a slight nod. She handed him the key card and told him how to get to his room.

"I notice you don't have a check out date written down here."

"I'm not sure yet. I'll let you know."

The man, who signed the register as Tom Hardman, stepped into an empty elevator nearly collapsing from fatigue. It had taken him an entire day to get here. The trip had been a long, grueling one from his island paradise to his final destination, but he had arrived. He was finally in Los Angeles.

CHAPTER 8

Dana's first hint that something significant had happened was when there was a loud knock on the ladies room door.

"Mrs. Mansfield, come quick!" There was urgency in Agent Conway's voice.

With her heart pounding, she raced from the bathroom in time to catch a glimpse of him disappearing into her office. As she followed him, Dana whispered a fervent prayer.

"Lord, please, please, please," was all she could think of to say.

When she entered her office, everyone was gathered around the computer. She could hear someone on the screen talking. She stepped further into the room and James' gray eyes were the first pair that she met. They were shining. He had a big grin on his face, but it was Agent Conway who delivered the good news.

"They're free."

One of the agents in Carmel was on screen looking harried and talking frantically to Agent Conway. It seemed that he was having quite a bit of difficulty containing the Stewart and Reasoner families, who insisted on seeing their children right away. Dana wanted to be on the Peninsula with her family, but she had to be content with seeing everything that was happening there in real time.

The joy that permeated the household with Gillian's telephone call was evident even in L.A. After getting the call, Sin put Gillian on speaker phone, and she explained how she and Nia made it to safety.

Having escaped their captors, the girls made their way to the home of a family of farmers who spoke limited English. Gillian's Spanish lessons came in handy as she explained their plight to them. The family let her use their telephone to call her father. With as much accuracy as possible, Gillian told Sin where they were located, and he assured her that they would be there ASAP. Sin also instructed her to stay on the phone with him until they got to her.

The two overwrought couples were headed for a car to go rescue their daughters when the agents stopped them, and informed the parents that the authorities could not allow them to go alone. The situation had to be checked out. But, rationale in the face of emotion proved fruitless. All hell broke loose. Both set of parents demanded to be taken to their children. A war of words had ensued and a firestorm was brewing on the Peninsula as the agent was on screen explaining the situation to the agents in L.A., the heated argument in the background was loud and clear. Dana wasn't surprised when an enraged Darnell pushed the agent aside and appeared on screen to speak to her aunt.

"Dana, you're my attorney and you had better tell these people something!" She was so angry that her voice was shaking. "I will personally sue the FBI, and have every one of these damn agents fired if they don't let us out of here."

Agent Conway addressed the emotionally spent mother. His tone was sympathetic.

"Like I said, Mrs. Stewart, we'll be happy to take all of you by helicopter to wherever you want to go, but we do have to think about your safety and that of the children. We *must* secure the area first."

The stare that Darnell leveled him with was deadly.. "Am I talking to you?"

Dana recognized her niece's need to get to her child, but she also understood the FBI's position. "Let the authorities do their job, Hon. You'll be with Nia soon."

Issuing that directive was difficult. Dana had to swallow her emotions. Switching to a professional persona wasn't easy after the roller coaster ride that they had all been on. When Darnell's eyes narrowed in rejection of that advice, Dana prepared herself for the onslaught of opposition that she knew was coming, but Thad came to the rescue.

"Nia wants to speak to you again," he told his wife. He handed her Sin's cell phone and immediately, Darnell's focus turned to their little girl.

While Agent Conway continued to direct the rescue mission, Dana slipped into a deserted conference room. She barely made it inside before she burst into tears. She didn't hear the door open and close quietly behind her, but she did feel his presence when James turned her around to face him and eased her against the comfort of his massive chest.

"Let it go," he whispered. She did.

Heaving sobs shook her body as he became a silent witness to her personal pain. James knew that what he stumbled into by accident might possibly be the news story of the year. Yet, this very private moment would never be revealed.

When he woke up yesterday morning, never, in his wildest imagination, would he have thought of this scenario. How could anyone?

During the time he spent engulfed in this unexpected drama, he tried to be unobtrusive as he silently assessed all of the characters involved. They each proved to be very interesting.

There was Agent Conway, the ambitious company man, who knew that if this case ended successfully there would be no obstacles on his way to the top. James only caught a brief glimpse of Ray Wilson's wife, Bev. He never met her, but he knew her husband well enough to know that although he might be a hard-nosed, wheeler dealer on the Hollywood scene, Ray was also a kind and considerate man. James doubted that he would choose a wife who wasn't the same.

James was aware that Thad Stewart was not only Ray's client, but his best friend, and Darnell was Ray's step-daughter. James had no doubt that because of Ray's close relationships with those in the Stewart family, the entire kidnapping scenario had to tear him apart.

James had never met Thad or Darnell, but from what he was able to discern from afar, Thad's personality appeared to be less intense than that of his wife's. While the super star actor was laid back, it was clear that Darnell was a warrior who would wage battle until the end.

Nedra Reasoner had stayed in the background through this ordeal. James hadn't seen much of her, but he was curious about what type of woman Sinclair Reasoner married. In spite of his nemesis' role as a worried father, seeing Sin continued to evoke bitter feelings in James, feelings that he thought were buried long ago. He was wrong. He still hated the man.

The feel of Dana stirring in his arms brought James' thoughts back to the moment. Through all of this, she was the one whom he came to know best. Despite their rocky start he liked her. She not only had heart, but she had *a* heart, as her tears demonstrated.

Composing herself, Dana drew away from him. She was embarrassed by her emotional outburst.

"I'm really sorry about this. It all came down on me at once."

"No problem. You've been through a lot."

She smiled in appreciation. Who would have thought that this giant of a man would have such a gentle spirit?

They returned to her office in time to see the families leaving with the agents to go pick up the girls. It was like watching a movie—the ride to the helicopter, and the quartet of anxious parents hopping aboard the aircraft.

It didn't take long before it was landing in an open field close to a ramshackle house located in the middle of an onion field. The parents leaped to the ground before the pilot turned the engine off. They sprinted across the field toward the house which the agents had secured. Suddenly, two small figures darted from behind a group of uniformed officers and raced toward the quartet. Reaching their parents, each girl leaped into open arms, and was greeted with hugs and kisses. It was a moment in which, no one in Carmel or L.A. hid their emotions.

Dana turned to Agent Conway, "I need to get to Carmel, *today*."

****

"I'll say that you'll be lucky if you have eight hours to get ahead of the media, if that."

The warning was being given by Brandon Plaine to the gathering that filled the Reasoner's spacious living room. Sin called him as soon as they returned home with Gillian and Nia. There was no doubt as to who would get the exclusive on the story of the kidnapping. The media mogul owned media outlets nationwide. Yet, at the moment, his presence among those who knew and trusted him as a friend was personal. He and his wife, Sash, knew the horror of what the families had endured. They also knew what could help them recover from their ordeal.

"The best advice that I can give you," Brandon told them, "is to disappear. Public scrutiny isn't what you need right now . Stay out of the spotlight. "

"I'll call Uncle Gerald to fly his plane here and pick us up," Bev informed the others. That meant that within the next 24 hours every family member present would be in the security of the family compound in the town of Stillwaters, beyond the media's reach.

"Our house in Hawaii is up for grab," said Sash. She and her husband had agreed in advance to offer their vacation home on a private island as a sanctuary.

"Thank you," Nedra gave the couple a grateful smile. She knew where her family members would gather, so her eyes slid to the Stewart's housekeeper, who was also in the room. Darnell picked up on Nedra's nonverbal cue.

"What about you Mrs. Sharon? How would you like a vacation with pay?"

Shocked, Mrs. Sharon's hands flew to her mouth. "What?"

"You can even bring a family member or a friend along," Brandon urged.

Thad added, "All expenses paid."

"You've been to Pineapple Hill with us before, Mrs. Sharon," Darnell added, "You said that you liked it."

Mrs. Sharon choked back tears.. "But it was my fault that…"

"*Nothing* was your fault," Thad interrupted. "You did all that you could."

Mrs. Sharon was moved to tears. Despite all efforts to make her feel differently the Stewart's trusted housekeeper felt responsible for what happened to the girls. She had been despondent. But she perked up at the show of love and support.

"It'll be fun," Marva prodded.

"If Brandon and Sash don't mind, Sin and I can call Mrs. Lucia to see if she might want to go to the island too," said Nedra.

"No problem at all," said Brandon.

Mrs. Sharon looked excited by the possibility. She and Mrs. Lucia were good friends, but she remained hesitant.

"I think the authorities still suspect me of something. Suppose Agent Conway says that I can't go?"

Darnell rolled her eyes and snorted. "Don't worry. I'll take care of him."

With that reassurance, Mrs. Sharon accepted the invitation. Everyone in the room was pleased, especially Darnell. Mrs. Sharon was working for her long before Thad and Nia came into her life. As far as she was concerned the woman was above reproach.

"Okay, that's settled," said Carla Ryan-Belle, who was presiding over the gathering. "It sounds like everybody should be out of the reach of the media and the paparazzi."

Nedra had called her best friend on their return home with the girls. A few hours later, Carla, her husband Jacob, and their twins were on the Reasoner's doorstep.

Carla owned a Public Relations agency in Berkeley. She was skilled at handling the media. The families decided that when the news of the kidnapping broke, she would serve as their spokesperson.

As Dana sat among the others, she was buoyed by the feeling of euphoria that surrounding her. Like everyone present, she couldn't wipe the smile off of her face.

Before the meeting began, Nedra's mother had offered a rousing prayer of thanks for the safe return of the girls. Marva cited their escape as living proof of the power of prayer.

Dana couldn't disagree. Although she didn't attend church on a regular basis, her faith in the Almighty was strong. She was certain that some kind of divine intervention was responsible.

She was glad to be in Carmel with her family. It was Agent Conway who invited her to join him on his flight to the Peninsula. He was going there to assess the situation. Dana asked if James could accompany them.

"He was headed to northern California when he got blindside by everything that happened here," she reminded the agent.

Conway agreed, and James accepted the offer. Dana wanted James to meet her family members, but he declined.

"I've got too much to do," was his excuse.

The plane dropped him off in San Francisco before taking her to the Monterey Peninsula. Dana and James bid each other goodbye at the airport. They exchanged business cards with promises to keep in touch, even though they weren't sure if that would happen.

By the time Dana arrived at the Reasoner home, the girls had been debriefed and were asleep together in Gillian's room. Dana rushed upstairs to see them. They were snuggled up together in Gillian's bed. Tears streamed down Dana's face at the sight of them lying safe and content.

Downstairs where everyone was assembled, Dana was provided with the details of the girls' escape. Gillian emerged as the heroine.

"She covered the fact that her and Nia escaped so well that the agents said it probably took the kidnappers a while to discover that they were gone," Bev crowed.

"That's my baby!" Sin proudly bellowed.

"And my niece!" Darnell and Sin gave each other a high five.

Every person in the room was elated. One of their own delivered a blow to crime. The story about their little she-ro was repeated like a mantra.

"You should have seen her, Dana!" Nedra's eyes were glowing. "When we picked them up Gillian was so mad that she wanted to go to the house with the FBI, and I quote…"

"Kick some butt!" The two sets of parents said in unison.

"We had to drag her away from there," said Sin. His eyes met his wife's eyes. Their transition from the deepest despair to this absolute high in such a short time was astonishing.

Dana's heart was full as she got caught up in the euphoria. "So she knew exactly where the kidnap house was located?"

It was Thad's turn to brag about his niece. "Would you believe that the little rascal left a trail of rocks and twigs along the way which lead right back to the house?" .

"The officers said that nobody would have really noticed them if she hadn't used them as markers." Like everyone else in the room Sin was in awe of his daughter's ingenuity. "On top of that she wrote a detailed description of the house for the authorities."

Dana was impressed. "The kid's a genius."

"And we're never going to hear the end of it," Colin, piped in.

Trevor groaned. "She'll be bragging about this for the rest of her life."

Her brothers' comments were said in jest, but there was truth behind the words. It was well known that modesty was not one of Gillian's strong points.

Dana was bursting with pride. "She's a Stillwaters, that's for sure."

There were no denials. They were from a family that instilled tenacity in their children. Gillian had learned her lesson well.

The remainder of the afternoon was spent planning the families' exodus to the Stillwaters homestead where they could be assured privacy. Dana planned to go with them.

"We've got to increase the town's security, especially since the kidnappers are still out there," Sin noted

"Yeah," Thad agreed. "We need to hire a good security firm to make sure our houses are secure while we're gone."

As soon as the words left his mouth, Dana and Ray exchanged a look. She put their thoughts into words.

"I know exactly who we can get to do the job."

****

When the cell phone on the night stand rang, James was asleep. He was so exhausted that he could hardly raise his head off of the pillow. After arriving at his hotel room, he showered and went straight to bed. Although he had been asleep for hours, it felt as though he just fell asleep enough.

Groping for the intrusive instrument, he hoped it wasn't a work emergency. He'd had enough excitement over the past 48 hours.. His voice sounded like gravel when he answered the call.

"Hello?"

"I need you."

James sat straight up. He recognized Dana's voice.

"Tell me when and where."

CHAPTER 9

It was the muffled voices that woke him up. Groggy, the man who registered at the L.A. hotel as Thomas Hardman, let the sound settle into his consciousness. He hoped that the voices would go away, but they grew louder. He opened his sleep laden eyes and traced the source of the annoyance to the door that stood as a barrier between his room and the one next to his.

When he checked into this mid-priced hotel, he did so to avoid the possibility of bumping into anyone who might have known him in the past. The circles in which he used to socialize wouldn't be caught dead in a place like this. It wasn't a fleabag, but it wasn't luxurious either. He figured it would be filled with wide-eyed tourists excited about being in Los Angeles, and he planned on blending in as one of them.

Right now it sounded as though two of those tourists were next door arguing. From the sound of it they were right against the door that separated the rooms because their voices were no longer muffled. They were loud and clear. He could hear every word. Great! To top it off the boisterous duo were staying in a corner room which meant that he would be the only recipient of their noisy outrage.

"Man! We gotta get outta this town!" Voice #1 declared.

"I told you to calm down," Voice #2 demanded loudly. "Nobody knows who we are. We have a plan and we're going to stick to it."

"A plan that's going to get us caught!" Voice #1 sounded desperate.

Caught? Hardman lifted up on his elbows. It sounded as though he had ended up in a hotel containing more than tourists.

"Caught with what?" Voice #2 sounded incredulous. "We didn't go to the drop site…"

Drop site? What were they talking about? Drugs?

"Because those damn kids got away!" voice #1 shrilled angrily.

"You're right about that," growled Voice #2. "We should have killed them both!"

Huh? It didn't sound like drugs. Fluffing his pillow behind his back, Hardman propped himself up.

"Man you're talking crazy!" Voice #1 screamed.

"No, I'm not crazy," Voice #2 barked menacingly.

"But getting rid of them would have been a major mistake." Voice #1 sounded certain. "Right now, we're home free. We don't have any money that anybody can trace…"

"You got that right!" Voice #2 spat bitterly. "And since there's no evidence and nobody knows who we are, we'll stick to the plan. Go back to work as if nothing happened and keep your mouth shut."

Voice #1 uttered an expletive, "Let go of me! You ain't runnin' nothin'. I'm outta here!"

There was a loud thump against the wall that separated the rooms. Hardman assumed that one of the men threw the other one against it. The wall shook. Whatever was said next was muffled. Hardman could only imagine that Voice #2 was issuing Voice #1 a threat. He'd witnessed the scenario many times. He'd issued intimidating threats himself. His only concern was that if something illegal had occurred involving these two jokers, the authorities might show up and he didn't need that. Maybe he picked the wrong hotel to stay in after all.

Yawning, Hardman stretched and scooted down on the bed. His entire body felt like lead. Exhaustion had claimed him earlier and he had fallen asleep as soon as his head hit the pillow. Glancing at the clock by his bedside he wondered if the time he saw could be right. If so, he had slept for nearly 24 hours.

Answering Mother Nature's call, he stumbled to the bathroom, took a shower, and brushed his teeth. When he returned to the bedroom it was quiet next door. The issue between his feuding neighbors was either settled or maybe they had checked out. He hoped it was the latter.

While he was ironing his clothes, he decided to turn on the TV. A news channel was on, and a familiar voice drifted from the set.

"This is to the people who had the audacity to touch our child."

Hardman's head snapped up. He gawked at the television screen. Darnell Cameron stared back at him.

"The FBI is hot on your trail, but they should be the least of your worries."

He stilled. *What's going on?* Darnell glowered at the screen through narrowed slits .

"If they don't find you, rest assured that we will." Thad's jaw was tight. His well-dressed form was stiff with rage.

Abandoning his ironing, Hardman perched on the end of the bed directly in front of the TV screen, giving it his undivided attention. The camera was focused on a tight shot of the famous singer as she looked into the camera.

"The federal government might run out of time and money to put into tracking you down, but we won't. We've got more than enough of both to hire the best detectives in the world to find you, and we will. So my advice is for you is to turn yourself in to the authorities, because believe me, you will fare much better with them. If you choose not to, I swear to you that as long as you walk this earth we will have people out there looking for you. We will track you into hell if we have to, and we *will* find you." Darnell's voice deepened. "That's a promise."

He leaned closer. What was this about? The camera returned to the two news anchors.

"That was a pre-recorded statement from superstars Darnell Cameron and Thad Stewart. The message is addressed to the person or persons who days ago kidnapped their five year old daughter, Nia, and her eleven year old cousin, Gillian Reasoner."

"What?" Hardman leaped to his feet.

"The girls escaped from their captors and the hunt for their abductors has been on ever since."

His heart pounded in his ears. It seemed as though he had slept through the news story of the year. Flipping from station to station, he found every channel inundated with details of the abduction and the escape.

There were pictures of the abandoned farm house in which the little girls were kept. Each station gave a tour of the house. They showed the tiny room in which the children had been kept and the bathroom window from which they escaped. One station re-enacted every moment, retracing the trail where Gillian Reasoner left indiscrete clues that led the FBI back to the house where she and her cousin were held captives.

The family that helped the girls was paraded before the cameras. The husband and wife were hailed as heroes, and it was announced that they would be presented with a substantial financial reward by the girls' grateful parents.

Between commercials, Hardman scanned social media to see if he could find more details about the crime. He was especially eager to find photos of the kidnapped children, or their parents.

When he returned to the news channel it was reporting that the Stewarts and the Reasoners had gone into seclusion. Their spokesperson informed the media that no photos of the girls would be released and that there would be no interviews with them or with family members. Hardman was disappointed.

As evening descended, he ordered his meal from room service, not daring to move from his spot in front of the TV, fearing he might miss something. Later that evening he ventured out to find a newsstand and purchased a copy of every publication containing the kidnap story.

Going through newspaper meticulously, he found plenty of old pictures of Darnell and Thad, but there was only one faint photo of Sinclair Reasoner that he could find. It offered a grainy glimpse of his profile as he was entering a building. It seemed that there had been some sort of scandal years ago involving him and some drug cartel. At the time, his reported lover was the pastor of a church in Oakland, who was also a noted anti-drug activist. The woman was now his wife.

Hardman raised an eyebrow at that bit of information as he studied a picture of Nedra Davis Reasoner posing regally in her religious garb. She was classy and she was a beauty. This Sinclair guy had good taste. The couple had three adopted children. The little girl who was abducted was the youngest.

Hardman was disheartened as he scoured every media source available. There were no pictures of the Reasoner children or of Nia Cameron-Stewart anywhere. ..

He was engrossed in reading about the abduction when he heard the door to the room next door open and close. There was the muffled sound of voices, but they were more subdued this time.

He sighed in disgust. Hopefully, it wasn't the quarrelsome duo. If he was lucky new occupants were in the room. If not, he hoped the battling bozos had settled their dispute so that he could get some rest. It wasn't until much later that he remembered what their heated discussion was about.

****

"The crowd outside of the gate is growing," James reported to Dana as he patrolled the perimeter of the Reasoner property located high above the Pacific Ocean. "It's wild out there."

It had been forty-eight hours since the story of the kidnapping reached the media, and the frenzy was on. Dana's brother-in-law, Ray, volunteered to stay behind to help in any way that he could while James secured the homes of both families.

Ray was staying at the Cameron-Stewart home. He had invited James to set up his temporary quarters there as well.

As a couple, Darnell and Thad shunned the bright lights of Hollywood. They lived a quiet life on the Monterey Peninsula in the picturesque town of Carmel-by-the-Sea. The road that led to the cul-de-sac where they lived was obscured by a grove of trees. The road was nearly undetectable to anyone unfamiliar with the area. The high gate at the street's entrance served as a barrier to any invasion of their privacy. Yet in the wake of the publicity that followed the abduction, the media and paparazzi found the superstars' Shangri-La. The invaders were inventing all kinds of creative ways to break through the gate's protective barrier.

James was both pleased and surprised when his security company was hired to protect the Stewart and Reasoner properties. He pulled his most trusted personnel from their L.A. office to assist in the effort, but early indications were that he might have to fly in additional personnel from New York.

"It's a free for all out here," he told Dana. "The security company that patrols this neighborhood has their hands full outside the gate. My people are discretely stationed inside the cu-de-sac."

What he didn't tell her was that every employee of the security company, that usually patrolled the cul de sac, was being investigated by the FBI to see if any of them might have been involved in the kidnapping. Keeping that company's personnel outside of the gates was part of a strategic plan. The authorities didn't want to arouse suspicion among the employees. His own company's personnel had already been vetted, and everyone was cleared by the FBI.

"Did you get Sin and Nedra's house secured yet?" Dana wanted to know.

She was referring to the motion lights that James recommended be installed on the Reasoner property. While he found the Stewart property secure, with its high, gated, wall and state of the art monitoring system, the Reasoner house proved more accessible. Only the bluff high above the sea at the back of the house, where he presently stood, offered an obstacle for potential trespassers. The rest of the property was vulnerable.

"It's being secured as we speak," James told her. "The only problem that we have is those blasted news helicopters flying overhead." He looked up in time to see yet another one headed his way. He groaned into the receiver, "Speaking of the devil."

As he spoke, James started walking toward the house. He wanted to enjoy the spectacular ocean view, but that wasn't to be. While the trees lining the grounds kept the copters from landing, the bold invaders got close enough to make a lot of noise. Dana could hear the racket on her end of the phone line.

"And how is Ray holding up?" There was a hint of amusement in her inquiry. Dana knew that despite having been married for a couple of years, Bev and Ray still acted like amorous newlyweds. They hated being apart. Her sister, who was in Stillwaters with the rest of the family, was complaining about missing him. She wondered if Ray was expressing the same sentiment. From the chuckle on the other end, she guessed the answer.

"If you mean is he bugging me about getting this over with so that he can get back to Bev, then he's not holding up very well. As a matter of fact, if he doesn't stop whining I'm going to strangle him."

Dana laughed. She really liked this man.

As James walked to the front of the Reasoner house and headed down the long driveway, he thought the same thing about Dana. This sophisticated, highly intelligent woman with the superstar relatives wasn't haughty. During the short time that they spent together in her office, he found her to be quite down to earth. After they parted, he wasn't sure if he would hear from her again, but he was certainly glad that he did.

When she called to hire his company for their services, initially he was elated. Not only was it an excellent business opportunity, but there was the possibility of seeing the delectable Mrs. Mansfield again. However, his exhilaration was short-lived when she informed him of his expected duties. He realized that his employers would not only be the Stewarts, but the Reasoners. The thought of working for someone he hated as much as Sinclair Reasoner nearly made him decline the offer.

He conferred with his partner, who threatened to dissolve the partnership if he let emotions overshadow a business decision. Assuring himself that the bad blood between Sin and him wasn't going to interfere with his ability to do the job, he deferred to his partner. He called Dana back to accept the offer with the realization that something more important was at stake than a grudge between two grown men—and their names were Nia and Gillian.

"How are the girls?" he asked.

Like most of the country, James was still marveling at the spunk displayed by the two children. Having inadvertently shared some of the intense drama in their young lives, he felt a connection to them.

"Miss Gillian is strutting around here like the queen of the universe. She's the conquering heroine as far as everyone in our family is concerned and she's eating it up. Nia is still her sweet little self. She's just happy to be back with her Mommy and Daddy. I think she's too young to understand the magnitude of what happened to them."

James didn't want to admit it, but he was curious about Sin's private life. He had hoped that the man would be dead by now, not living in a custom built mansion complete with a swimming pool, a tennis court and a guest house all nestled high above the Pacific Ocean.

In the beautifully decorated house, James viewed the pictures of Sin's attractive wife and their three children. It had been difficult to suppress the anger he felt at seeing this happy family unit. It was a painful reminder of all that he had lost.

James also learned that Sinclair Reasoner owned his own business, and was a very wealthy man. He had hit the jackpot in every way. Knowing that served to enhance his intense loathing of the man. However, those feelings didn't extend to one specific member of the man's extended family.

"Now I'd like to ask you something, Mrs. Mansfield. When am I going to see you again?" There was no doubt that he wanted that to happen. "Usually I don't mix business with pleasure, but technically I don't work for you. So, when are you coming out of hiding?" Like everyone else in the country, he had no idea where any of Dana's family members were staying.

"I can assure you that you will be the first to know," she teased.

One week later, Dana's words proved to be prophetic.

CHAPTER 10

As Dana and Sin turned onto the street where the house in Tiburon, California was located she didn't want to seem too excited about seeing James again. The house belonged to Ray. He lived there before marrying her sister and it was now available for lease. Bev and her husband currently resided on a luxurious house boat in nearby Sausalito. Presently, the furnished house was unoccupied and had been selected as a perfect meeting place for James and her to meet because of its secluded location. The media was unaware of its existence.

The kidnapping was still the hottest topic in the country. Because of this the Stewarts and the Reasoner families remained in Stillwaters, their hometown sanctuary.

It was there that their large extended family gathered to support their loved ones. Lots of emotion was expended, including apprehension about the welfare and safety of the entire Stillwaters clan. The kidnapping had been a jolt to everyone.

Members of Dana's prosperous, extended family were raised to think of themselves as invincible. That illusion was shattered when Gillian and Nia were snatched.

The Stillwaters started their week together with a family meeting. There were close to three hundred people in attendance, all needing the reassurance of those closest to them that they were safe. The love and affection they felt for each other was evident. Still, there was tension among them.

Dana's widowed mother, Ginny Little, was the head of the large Stillwaters clan. A retired heart surgeon, it was her responsibility to keep the family together and to guard its privacy. It wasn't easy to do.

Many members of the Stillwaters clan graced the covers of some of the country's major publications, with Darnell and Thad being the most visible. The family's collective wealth was vast, making its members targets. What happened to Nia and Gillian was the family's worse nightmare, and some of its members took issue with how the girls' parents were handling the search for the kidnappers.

At the meeting, one of Darnell's cousins challenged her. "I don't think that issuing a statement baiting the abductors is the way to do this. It might bring unwarranted attention to the family as a whole!"

Taking center stage, Darnell disagreed. "While I can appreciate your observation, my husband and I have no intention of letting those baby snatchers have any peace. I want to make sure every day that they walk this earth is a day they walk in fear of being caught. I'm sorry if anybody here has a problem with that, but that's the way it's going to be. I want the kidnappers and everybody else to know I meant what I said and I said what I meant. They're never going to get away with this!"

Her words had brought a round of cheers from nearly everyone in the room. Dana and Bev exchanged proud grins. Darnell always had spunk. They knew there would be no backing down.

Dana's cousin, Gerald Stillwaters, Jr.—better known as Scott—shouted out angrily. "Jail is too good for the kidnappers! Nobody touches a Stillwaters!"

The family roared in agreement. Filled with righteous indignation Scott gave a stirring speech about their ancestors and the legacy of strength and courage that each member of their family inherited from them. "What is the motto of the Stillwaters clan?" he bellowed.

"Family First!" came the thunderous reply from every man, woman and child in the room.

"That's right!" Scott continued, sounding like a preacher at a church revival. "Loyalty is to our own and justice will prevail!"

It took Ginny Little's quiet persuasion to calm the raucous brood. After the room settled down, she reassured her family that things would turn out as they should. The abductors would be caught. That declaration ended the discussion and the meeting.

Dana was proud of the respect her mother garnered as the family's matriarch. Her wisdom and grace helped the Stillwaters thrive as a cohesive unit. It was her guidance that had brought Dana to Tiburon.

After the general meeting, Ginny had gathered the Stewarts, the Reasoners, Dana and Bev together for a small summit. She wanted to know if the families had hired a private detective to track the kidnappers.

"That's my great-granddaughter and my grand niece that they snatched," Ginny declared angrily. "Whoever did this has got to go down!"

Dana couldn't help but smile when she remembered the look of resolve on her mother's face. It was at the gathering of the immediate family that Dana brought up the idea of hiring Web Starr Security Services to do that job too. No one had any objections, so she called James that very day.

Of course, Dana couldn't deny that she had ulterior motives for volunteering to personally deliver the paperwork to James for his signature. She wanted to see him again.

They spoke on the telephone nearly every day since his company was hired to secure the properties in Carmel, but both of them knew that was a farce. Until he expressed his desire to see her again, Dana hadn't been sure if he was interested in her. Now she knew.

Dana wasn't sure why Sin volunteered to accompany her back to California. He claimed that he had unfinished business in the Bay Area. Recalling the tension she witnessed between James and Sin, she was surprised when he asked to go with her, knowing that he might come face to face with James.

Dana hadn't questioned Sin about the animosity between the two men. She knew that Nedra's husband could be very self-contained. Over the years, getting to know him hadn't been easy. But, after the startling revelation that Sinclair Reasoner was Darnell's half brother, Dana made an extra effort to get to know him, and she came to the realization that he was quite a man.

To say that he was good looking was an understatement. Sin turned women's heads wherever he went, but that wasn't what defined him. It was his devotion to his wife, children and to Darnell and her family that Dana most admired. He was also fiercely loyal to his friends. It was certain that James wasn't among them, and she didn't know what to expect when the two men eventually ended up in the same room. She wasn't sure that she wanted to find out.

Parking the car, in front of the house in Tiburon, Sin turned to her. "Are you ready?"

Dana nodded, but she couldn't help but wonder if he was?

****

James stood on the balcony of Ray's house gazing at the view beyond. It was magnificent. The day was clear. He could see Angel Island, Alcatraz and beyond to the Golden Gate Bridge. Ray informed him that he had purchased the house from Thad Stewart before Ray married Bev. Since James was settling in northern California, Ray offered to lease the house to him. James was seriously considering the offer..

As he reveled in the serenity of the panorama in front of him, James couldn't help but reflect on the twists and turns in his life that had brought him to this point. As a young gang member in Harlem, he engaged in a lot of criminal activity and didn't expect to live beyond twenty-one. Now here he was, standing on the balcony of the former home of one of the biggest stars in the world, and he was considering this house as his future residence. He had come a long way. *If only Regina and Pookie were here.*

Turning away from the balcony, he closed his eyes against the pain of that memory. Unconsciously, his hand caressed the name tattooed on his bulging bicep.

He had to stop this! He forced the heartache of what happened to them into a corner of his subconscious decades ago, so that he could go on with his life. His efforts were successful until he saw Sinclair Reasoner again.

James gave himself credit for being able to put aside his emotions and accept the challenge of working for the man. The truth was that if it hadn't been for those two little girls, he would have passed on this job, whether his partner agreed or not.

James walked into the master bedroom. The plan was for him to spend the night in the house after his meeting with Dana and then tomorrow he would return to the Monterey Peninsula. Ray would be staying on his houseboat tonight, and then flying to be with his wife who was with the rest of the family, wherever that was.

"Dana's here!" Ray's voice came through the intercom.

James' heart lurched at the mention of her name. It had been a long time since that happened. He hadn't been interested in a woman for anything other than sex for years. When he was in his late twenties, he tried marriage, but that turned out to be a disaster. Since then he avoided close relationships, but there was something about the delectable Mrs. Mansfield that attracted him. He was elated at the prospect of seeing her.

Dana explained to him that she was bringing the contract to Tiburon in order to avoid the media and paparazzi camped out in front of the gate in Carmel. But, James was fully aware that their business could have been taken care of electronically, without face to face contact. Her bringing the contract to him personally meant she wanted to see him as much as he wanted to see her. Now she was here. He forced himself not to run down the stairs.

Dana greeted Ray when he opened the door.

"I'm not alone," she informed him. "Sin came with me. He's in the car making a phone call."

"That's fine, but how's Bev doing?"

Chuckling, Dana gave him an affectionate kiss on the cheek. "You ought to know. You talk to her ten times a day."

She liked the way that Ray loved her sister. As a couple they were devoted to each other. Seeing the two of

them together almost made her believe in love again—
almost.

Divorced twice and having buried a fiancée, Dana
wasn't sure that she could make it through another
relationship. But, then she looked up, saw James bounding
down the stairs and her heart did a flip-flop in her chest.
There was something about this man.

James was professional when he addressed Dana. Yet,
his grey eyes were sparkling.

"Hello, Dana. It's good seeing you again." Uncertain
about how to greet her, he stuck his hand out for a
handshake.

Dana looked from him to his hand and back again.
"You've got to be kidding!" Laughing at the formality, she
hugged his large frame.

Responding to her warm greeting, James inhaled the
fragrance she was wearing, recognizing it as the same one
she wore that day in her office when they first met.
Withdrawing from their embrace, his eyes swept her
shapely form. Dressed in jeans and a tee shirt, she looked
much different than the buttoned up business woman that
he first met.

He wanted to savor this moment of their reunion, but
Ray was standing there looking at them, and then the front
door opened. Sinclair Reasoner entered, holding a cell
phone to his ear. James stiffened.

The two men stared at each other. The tension
between them was instantly palpable. Sin turned his
attention to Dana and Ray.

"Agent Conway is on the line. They've picked up a
person of interest on the Peninsula. They're interrogating
him now."

****

The two battling strangers next door to Hardman had been on the move for a week. He had been watching them clandestinely and knew they would eventually split up. The fact that they didn't go their separate ways earlier indicated that they were amateurs. That proved to be a major advantage. Amateurs made more mistakes. They also made easy prey, especially for someone with experience in stalking prey. Although he might be a tad rusty, he *was* experienced.

It served him well when he opened the door between his room and that of his neighbors. He'd dare anyone to find any evidence that the lock had been picked. The swiftness with which he went through the few possessions that were in the room would have amazed its occupants. While there were toiletries and clothes packed in a couple of cheap suitcases, there was nothing to indicate their identities.

He knew what the men looked like. He made sure he could identify them the day he connected the argument he overheard with the abduction. It was on that day the two men became his prey.

He kept up with the progress of the kidnap investigation, reviewing media outlets daily. He purchased a burner cell phone, a mini video camera, the tools he used to break into the room next to him, and a small handgun, which, sadly, was much too easy to buy on the streets.

According to media reports, the authorities were close to identifying at least one of the abductors, and that was good. The pressure was on them to find the culprits quickly. Fans of Darnell Cameron and Thad Stewart were threatening vigilante justice. They were outraged that the lives of the beloved couple had been so violated, and so was Hardman. It made his blood boil, and fueled his need for revenge.

When he was a young hothead, the mere suspicion that the men next door might have touched those little girls would have meant instant death sentences for them both. Time had mellowed his impulsiveness. He wanted more evidence that what he suspected about them was true before he acted, so he watched and waited. If his suspicions were confirmed, only God could help them. He was always at his best when his motive was vengeance.

Two days after the abduction, the men checked out of the hotel, and so did he. Once outside the duo separated and he was faced with the dilemma of which one to follow.

The older of the two, a neatly dressed man in his late thirties or early forties, appeared to be quite self-assured. The other man, who looked to be in his late twenties, was more casual in his appearance. He was jumpy and less confident than his associate. Hardman knew instantly which one he would pursue.

That was a week ago, and he had ended up in the city of Inglewood, near the L.A. airport, where the man appeared to live alone in a small, boxlike house secured by burglary bars on every window and security doors on the front and back entrances. It looked like an, impenetrable fortress, but Hardman knew from experience that there was no such thing.

He checked into a hotel room not far from the house. How long he would be there depended on his skittish quarry, and when he would make a move.

The first day that Hardman observed him, the only trip the man made outside was to the grocery store. The second day that he followed him, Hardman hit the jackpot. The man turned out to be employed in a high rise in downtown Los Angeles. From the uniform he was wearing it was obvious that he was some sort of service worker, which proved to be significant when Hardman checked the roster of companies in the building. The name of one of the offices he recognized—Mansfield Legal Services—the firm owned by Darnell's Aunt Dana. That was all of the proof that Hardman needed. He had the right man.

When he wasn't observing his prey or following the progress of the authorities on the kidnap case, Hardman spent his time doing research at the library. Using the public computers, he sought all of the information he could find on the man whose existence prompted him to leave the safety of his island paradise. He wanted to find out about Sinclair Reasoner.

There was plenty that he already knew about Darnell Cameron. For years he devoured every tidbit of information he could find about her. It wasn't difficult, she was world renowned. Finding information about her so-called half brother proved to be more of a challenge.

The press identified Bayland Imports as the company owned by Sinclair Reasoner. The business website was informative, but there was little about its founder. He seemed to keep a low profile. Other than the scandal of years ago involving his relationship with his future wife, there was nothing else on Sinclair, not even a clear photo. Except for the brief glimpse of him that Hardman saw on TV, he didn't have a real semblance of the man about whom he was so curious.

Who was this man? What did he look like? Where did he come from?

With each visit he left the library feeling disappointed. He still didn't have any of the answers for which he had risked everything to come here and find. He harbored doubts about this man's claim of kinship to Darnell. The article he read on the island said something about DNA having verified the relationship, but damn that! He wanted absolute proof that what was being claimed was true.

Arriving back at the hotel from his visit to the library on this day, Hardman's spirits were lifted by the headline that a person of interest in the kidnapping case was being detained for questioning. The photo of the man confirmed that it wasn't the partner of the man that he was following. Hardman wondered if the man in custody was connected to the other two.

Normally, he was a patient man, but not in this case. If he was on the wrong track, he needed to know it. Yet, too many things added up for this joker he was following not to be involved in this kidnapping case,

After assessing the situation he considered several options. One particular one was especially appealing to him and became even more so with each passing day.

CHAPTER 11

"Man, this is major," James told his partner. Standing in the garden outside of the house in Tiburon he was enjoying the view of the San Francisco Bay. It seemed that no matter where he was in this house there was a breathtaking vista. There was no way that he was going to turn down Ray's offer to rent this place.

On the other end of the line, Nathan Webb gave a deep sigh. "Well, this is what we do track people down, that is if given a chance to do our job. What do you know about this guy that the FBI has in custody?"

"He's one of the security guards that patrols the street where the families live."

"That shouldn't have come as a surprise. I'm sure he was privy to schedules and personal telephone numbers for emergencies. Do any of the family members know the man?"

"No, not personally."

Nate snorted. "It doesn't sound like professionals planned this one. I would think that even amateurs would know that the security firm would be one of the first places the authorities would look for suspects. I don't know how many people were involved in this, but the FBI is probably hot on their trail as we speak." Pausing, James could hear Nate thinking even over the telephone. "I don't want to step on any toes. What else can we do to enhance their investigation?"

"The Stewarts and the Reasoners seem to think that we can do something. None of the families want this to turn into a cold case."

"I doubt that the Feds will let that happen. What other inside information do you have about the perp?"

James could hear a note of uncertainty in Nathan's voice. Neither one of them wanted to take on an assignment that might not offer their clients the best results. This was a high profile endeavor and if they faltered in any way it could damage their business reputation.

"The families were told, privately, that the man's name is Jack Spencer. Other than that the authorities didn't provide any more information about him. Agent Conway said they'll be releasing his name to the public soon."

"All right, and you're sure they still want to hire us despite the arrest?"

"According to Dana Mansfield. She was the one who drew up the contract that I sent to you."

Nathan sighed again. "I looked it over, and I also heard that statement that Darnell Cameron made. She didn't pull any punches, and there was subtext in what she had to say. I know what the contract says, but you did re-emphasize to their attorney that if we do find more suspects that all information will be turned over to the proper authorities, right?"

"I did, and I also told her that if our actions interfere with the Fed's investigation that we might have to re-evaluate our efforts."

"Well put. What did she say to that?"

"She said that she wouldn't expect any less from highly skilled professionals." James smiled as he remembered how much the compliment pleased him. "They just want them caught ASAP."

"They pay well, that's for sure."

Nate was right. Their agency was being offered a small fortune for its services. The reward being offered to the public for information leading to the arrest of the kidnappers had been raised to a staggering amount.

"We wanted to grow the business," his partner reminded him. "Ask and ye shall receive. I'm coming out there personally to help you with this one. When will the families be back on the Peninsula?"

"Not soon. Wherever they are both families plan to stay there until the press dies down. They said that they'll make the kids available for an interview with us if it's needed. I doubt if the FBI will be happy that we're on the case. They weren't thrilled with the statement that Darnell issued."

"She doesn't seem to be the type that would care."

"I think you're right."

Before disconnecting, the two men talked strategy and made plans for Nate to fly to California. They would have a lot of work to do tracking the kidnappers down, but. neither man had any doubts that they were up to the task.

James knew that merging his business with that of his friend's business had been a good move. Nathan Webb had been one of the best detectives in the New York City Police Department. He was also James' mentor.

James was a street hardened kid headed for jail, or hell, when the crime hardened cop took an interest in him. Nathan Webb was the father figure that he needed, when he needed one. James loved and respected him. He felt fortunate to have Nate in his life.

James was deep in thought about the job ahead of them when he felt a presence nearby. He turned. It was Dana.

"Did you talk to your partner?" She sat down on the redwood bench beside him.

"Yes."

Dana smiled. "Great! I bet you're quite a gum shoe."

"Gum shoe?" James laughed. "Where did you get that from, an old movie?"

"Sure, and from what I see on television being a private investigator is exciting and full of adventure."

James shook his head. "No, it's mostly tedious research and lots of interviewing. Nate is a master at both. He's the lead P.I., and I assist him as needed. My real expertise is security. He'll be flying out here soon and you'll get to meet him. I told him we have permission to interview the girls. By the way, how are they?"

Dana's smile widened. She liked James' concern for others. He really seemed to care.

"One of our cousins is a psychologist and she's having sessions with them. Nia is having nightmares, and Gillian is suspicious of everybody. She's quite a kid, but I'm afraid this ordeal has really been traumatic. Believe it or not, her best friend, Trent Plaine, was kidnapped when he was younger. Nedra says that they're in constant contact comparing notes, and as strange as it might seem, she says it appears to be therapeutic."

"Sounds good."

James was glad that the children were getting help, but, at the moment there was something else on his mind. From the moment the sexy attorney sat down beside him, his body temperature bega rising, among other things..

Dana pretended not to notice the effect their being close was having on James. She kept talking.

"Family members came from all over to celebrate the girls' return. We combined Gillian's twelfth birthday party with a welcome back celebration for them both. There was a huge cake with both of their names written across it, topped with twelve lit candles for Gillian. The girls went wild. They were so delighted. I mean we partied long and hard."

James chuckled. "You Stillwaters sound like a gang to me,"

"I guess we do." Dana hadn't thought of her family in those terms, but maybe he was right. "We are loyal to each other and we protect our own."

"And how about you, Mrs. Mansfield, are you in need of personal protection?" Flashing a sultry smile, he placed an arm across the back of the bench and stretched his long legs out in front of him.

Leaning back, Dana cocked her head. "Mr. Starr, are you flirting with me?"

James grinned. "That was my intention. I'm attracted to you."

Searching his compelling eyes, Dana noticed that they had darkened. She also sensed in him the same uncertainty that she was feeling, but she couldn't deny the truth.

"I'm attracted to you too."

"So what are we going to do about it?"

Dana shrugged. "I'm not sure."

"Then let's see if we can start with this."

Slowly, he lowered his lips to hers, offering Dana the chance to pull away. She didn't. Instead, she lifted her face to meet his. The kiss they shared was as gentle as it was thorough as their tongues explored and tantalized.

Dana gave a contented moan. This man knew what he was doing. She drew closer. His tongue delved deeper.

"Hey, Dana! Are you..."

Ray stopped short. Startled, Dana and James jumped apart.

"Oh! Sorry." Ray turned abruptly and headed back toward the house.

"Wait," Dana called after him. She was embarrassed that her brother-in-law caught her necking with a man that she barely knew, especially since James was a friend of his, but this was her business not his. She turned to Ray. "Did you need me for something?"

Ray looked at her steadily, noting her discomfort. He didn't understand why. Hell! She was an adult and so was James.

"I'm going to head over to the boat now. Are you going with me? You're kind of stranded. Sin took off to take care of some business."

Dana's plan was to stay on the houseboat overnight. Her Uncle Gerald, who had flown them to Marin County, was to return tomorrow to take them back to Stillwaters.

"I'll be right there."

Ray went back into the house. Dana turned to James.

"I guess we're busted," she said lightly.

James stood. "I guess. But I don't care." As he looked at this lovely woman, he wasn't sure that whatever there was between them could work, but he was drawn to her like a bee was to honey, and that was that.

"What would you say if we went on a date tonight?" Dana asked. "My treat. They have some great restaurants in Sausalito."

"Sounds like a plan to me."

Giving him a quick peck on the lips to seal the deal, Dana started walking toward the house, backwards. "Alright then, 7:00. I'll come and get you."

James nodded. "Okay."

With a two finger wave goodbye, she turned and went inside the house, leaving James standing in the colorful flower garden with the taste of her still on his lips.

****

Later that evening, it was a knock at the door that startled James awake. After Dana and Ray left he settled on the sofa in the family room and drifted off to sleep. It had been an exhausting day. A glance at the clock over the fireplace read a quarter to six.

Rubbing the sleep from his eyes, he knew that whoever was on the other side of the door must belong there. The wooden gate at the end of the sloped yard leading down to the street was locked. A key was needed to enter it. Figuring that it must be Dana coming early to pick him up for dinner, he padded barefoot across the room to answer the knock.

Looking through the peep hole he was shocked to see Sinclair Reasoner standing on the other side of the door. Excitement turned to anger. Hustling back to the family room, he retrieved his gun from its holster, tucked it in the back of his belt, covered it with his shirt and returned to the door.

Prior to this, distance and the presence of others stood between him and Sinclair. James was grateful for that, because if the two of them had been alone he wasn't sure if he would be responsible for his actions. It appeared that his resolve would now be tested. Reluctantly, he opened the door to the man that, years ago, he vowed to kill on sight.

CHAPTER 12

Without a word, James Starr stepped back and admitted Sin into the house. Sin's heartbeat quickened, not with fear, but with the thought of the years of animosity he had built up toward this man. He thought those feelings might have lessened by now, but the moment Starr's face appeared on the screen from Dana's office every suppressed emotion resurfaced.

"It was quite a surprise seeing you with Dana," he told his old nemesis, facing him, not daring to turn his back. "I thought you would be dead by now."

"I thought the same about you." James closed the door, positioning himself so that his back would not be turned to Sin. The lack of trust was mutual.

The two men studied each other. Physically, the years had been good to them both. They were each in their forties, still handsome and still fit. Of the two, Sin was more polished. The sharply creased slacks, the stylish jacket over a silk blend tee shirt and the soft, leather shoes on his feet all labeled him as being fashion conscious. James was still dressed in the cotton tee-shirt and faded blue jeans that he had worn since arriving in Tiburon that morning. His worn sneakers lay next to the sofa where he discarded them.

James and Sin were a study in contrast. Yet, their demeanors were exactly the same—hostile.

"My wife suggested that while I'm here I need to talk to you." Sin wasn't happy that she made him promise to follow-up on that suggestion, but he prided himself on being a man of his word.

A picture of Sin's wife flashed through James' mind. "Aw, yes, your wife, Nedra, I hear she's an ordained minister."

"Yes she is. She said that whatever is wrong between us is obvious. It makes everyone uncomfortable and we need to fix it."

"So that's why you're here." Still aware of Sin's every movement, James backed into the family room, sat down on the sofa and put his sneakers on. "To fix things." Tying his shoe laces, he gave Sin a hard look. "As if they can be fixed."

Sin shrugged. "What can I say? She's an optimist." He went to stand behind a chair located across from James.

"If she married you, she must be." James snorted derisively. "I can't believe it. *You*, married to a preacher. To say nothing about your claim to be Darnell Cameron's half brother. Are you kidding? What kind of scam are you pulling?" His voiced dripped with sarcasm.

Sin wasn't offended. He could understand James' skepticism, given the infamous past that they shared. Deception had been a part of life for them. Honesty was for suckers.

"Not that it's any of your business, but it's no scam. Darnell and I have the same father and there's a DNA test to prove it. But, that's neither here nor there. I came here to talk about us."

"What about us? I take it that your preacher wife knows about your past?"

"She does. I told her everything, even about our connection. I also told the authorities about how we know each other. I found out that you told them too, which was a surprise."

"They would have found out anyway." Rising, James walked to the fireplace and leaned against the mantel. He couldn't trust himself to be too close to this man. "Besides, the lives of two little girls were at stake. I didn't want them wasting their time on investigating me."

"That was good of you, and might I say that recording that guy's voice was quick thinking." Sin figured that James deserved credit for that at least.

As the seconds ticked by, there was an awkward silence. Despite the off-hand compliment, the tension in the room was still high..

The resentment that James felt toward Sin was eating him alive. He wasn't capable of having an intelligent conversation feeling like this. Seeing Sin standing there looking so prosperous galled him. He couldn't keep the bitterness out of his voice.

"I see that you've done well over the years, lots of money, a beautiful home, a classy wife and three good-looking kids."

"The last two things on the list are the most important."

"You don't say." James spat contemptuously. He wanted to whip his gun out and shoot him right on the spot. Sin had gone on with his life while his own life had been nearly destroyed.

Sin's jaw tightened at the scorn being directed his way. James made a sudden move toward him and Sin tensed, poised and ready to draw the gun concealed in its holster at the small of his back. Was this the moment their long running feud would boil over into physical conflict? He hadn't come here to fight, but he was prepared if it came to that. Undoubtedly, James was too.

Sin let out a breath that he didn't realize he had been holding when James' movements took him back to the sofa where he sat perched on the arm, but he continued to bait him

"I heard your children are adopted, but when I was at your house I saw a picture of your little girl. She looks a lot like you with that dimpled chin."

"Yes, I've been told," Sin answered calmly, aware of what James was insinuating.

He wouldn't be the first person to wonder if Gillian was his biological child. She wasn't, but the love that he felt for her and his sons was no less powerful. Because of this, he chose to ignore the veiled insult behind James' comment. Instead, he changed the subject. "How are Pookie and Regina?" He asked referring to James' son and the boy's mother.

James' jaws tightened. His nostrils flared. His eyes narrowed as he gave Sin a look that could kill. His hand slid to where his weapon lay nestled, ready to be pulled as he answered Sin's question in one harsh word.

"Dead."

Sin blinked. "What?"

When they were teenagers, James Starr was the war lord of the rival gang to which Sin belonged. The members of each gang earned their mantel as a men not only through fearless service to their brothers, but by their number of sexual conquests. Women were like chattel and the boys changed lovers regularly, except for James Starr. He had been devoted to a beauty named Regina Jason since they were both in grade school.

The relationship between the couple was solid.. James was a one woman man when it came to Regina. There wasn't another woman in Harlem who could say that they had slept with James Starr. He was a rare breed among his peers. A young man who was faithful to his lady,

"What happened?" Shocked, Sin didn't know what else to say. Regina would have been in her forties by now, and James, Jr., whose nickname was Pookie, would be in his twenties. "Were they in an accident or something?"

James leapt to his feet. Sin reached for his weapon. James reached for his. They stood frozen with their eyes locked; each waiting for the other to make a move that could prove deadly.

"You ought to know what happened!" James' voice trembled with rage. "It was you who had them killed!"

Sin was blindsided. He stared at him in astonishment.

"Are you crazy? What are you talking about?" Still poised to defend himself, Sin took a step back.

James' face was contorted with rage. He didn't need a gun to take this man's life. He could strangle him with his bare hands and watch with glee as the life seep from his body.

"After that hit from our gang took your guys down, we knew that you'd get your revenge, but never, in a million years did I think that my girlfriend and my son would have to pay the price. The woman I loved and my baby boy were shot down like animals right in front of my face!" A strangled sob caught in his throat.

Decades had passed since that night. The bullet wounds that ripped through his body had healed long ago, but the pain in his heart was just as raw as it had been on the day that he lost his family.

"Why man? " James thumped his chest with his fist in anguish. "Why *my* family?"

Sin sensed the danger in James' unbridled fury, but his own anger proved to be nearly as great. Undaunted, a defiant Sin moved from behind the chair to face the much larger man.

"I don't know what the hell you're talking about! I didn't have a thing to do with harming your family. Who said I did?" He didn't like liars or lies, especially when they were directed at him. "Hell! After I survived the ambush, I went straight to the bus station and headed out of New York!"

James shook his head in denial. "You're lying!" *He had to be.* "Bo Jack gave you up when we forced him to tell us who planned the hit on me that took out my family instead."

"Bo Jack told you a lie."

Sin's voice was steel. His eyes held James' fiery gray ones so that he could see the truth in what he was saying. There was a flicker of uncertainty in James' demeanor.

"But..." he frowned, bewildered. "But Bo Jack, said..."

"There are no *buts*," Sin snapped, reeling at the absurdity of the accusation. "I can prove where I was. I quit the gang the day that my friends were slaughtered. I haven't looked back since. I know I did a lot of bad things when I was a kid, but kill a woman and child?" Sin held up his hands, warding off the very thought. "No! No way!"

"He didn't say you pulled the trigger..."

"I bet he didn't..."

"He said that you planned it." The conviction in James' voice began to waver.

"How could I do that on a bus headed west?" Sin rubbed his hands across his face in frustration. Did the man not understand what he was saying? "I haven't seen or talked to Bo Jack since the day before the guys and I got ambushed." He whirled on James. "The ambush *you* planned!"

"What?" The disbelief in James' voice was as adamant as Sin's denial a few minutes ago.

"You were your gang's warlord!" He jabbed a forefinger toward James. "Who else would plan it?" Sin's bitterness was pronounced. "That gang was my family, man. The only one I'd ever known. Every one of those boys who died in that ambush was like a brother to me!"

Starr's responsibility for having planned the trap resulting in the deaths of Sin's fellow gang members put James on Sin's hate list to this very day. But, James shook his head vigorously.

"Man, you are so far off base." "I didn't have a thing to do with that. I didn't even know about that ambush until it was over."

"Yeah, I bet," Sin spat. "You were at the top of your gang's pyramid. It would have been impossible for you not to have been in on the planning."

James understood his skepticism. "My son came down with some kind of intestinal infection. I was with Regina in the hospital with him for three days straight. That hit was planned without me. I never found out who it was, but word was there was a traitor in your gang who told one of our foot soldiers when and where to find all of you together."

The two men looked at each other steadily. Both knew that whoever it was would have had something to gain by the deception. The answer came to both of them at once.

"Bo Jack." James whispered aloud. The same name was on Sin's mind.

Robert Jackson—known as Bo Jack—would have been the most likely member of Sin's gang to lead if his rivals were dead. The six boys who were ambushed by members of Starr's gang that fateful night would have been the ones who might have challenged Bo's rise to the top. His betrayal eliminated that possibility, but Sin survived to carry the memory of the carnage that he witnessed that night.

"Bo Jack didn't know that I left town, but he knew that there should have been six bodies." Sin's bitterness became redirected. "Since I didn't contact the gang, he probably thought that I was hiding out somewhere in the city."

"It was that bastard who butchered my family." James was beginning to see the light.

So was Sin. "What better way to get rid of me but to say I was responsible. Plus getting revenge on you after the ambush would have elevated his status in the gang."

"It was me that he was after. I was with my family." James closed his eyes to ward off the guilt and anguish that he had been carrying around with him for so long.

Sin watched James in silence, giving Starr the moment to feel the pain. He moved back to where he had been standing.

James took a shaky breath. "When we snatched Bo Jack..."

"You got him?"

"We snatched him butt naked, right out of bed at what he thought was a safe house. And with a little persuasion, he was more than willing to exchange your life for his. That's when he fingered you."

Sin raised an interested brow. "What happened to him?"

"Bo Jack's luck kicked in. My partner, Nathan Webb, saved his life. He saved mine too."

"How so?"

"Nate was part of the gang task force that burst in on us just before we put Bo out of his misery. They expected us to retaliate for my family and had us under surveillance. We were hauled in and they threw all kinds of charges at us. Nate felt sorry for me because of what happened to Regina and Pookie, and he took an interest in me. He kept in contact while I was serving time and when my mother died of cancer, he intervened for me so that I could attend her funeral."

"A cop with a heart." Sin leaned against the back of the chair. "I used to think that there was no such animal."

"The same here, but he did more than that. It was his vouching for me that got me released. Then he talked me into signing up for the Marine Corp."

That piqued Sin's interest. "You were in the service?"

"Yes."

"So was I, in the Army."

James perched on the arm of the sofa. "After I got out I joined the police force."

"Yeah, I heard about that." Sin sat down in the chair opposite him. "Did you ever find out what happened to Bo Jack?" He felt no guilt about what he hoped his answer would be. He wasn't disappointed.

"He was shanked in juvie," James reported. "Stabbed in the back."

"Good."

The culprit responsible for the death of both their families no longer walked the earth. Maybe now each man could find peace with the past.

With the tension between them lessened, the two men began to talk and discovered they had a lot in common. By the time Sin left the house a new respect for one another was evolving.

CHAPTER 13

"You're looking good, Mr. Starr," Dana complimented as he slid into the passenger seat of the car she was driving. He was wearing dark slacks and a knit shirt. On his feet he sported a pair of well shined shoes in place of his sneakers. He smelled good. "I see you went all out for our night on the town."

"Of course I did." James fastened his seat belt. "You wouldn't expect me to show up looking like a slob would you?" His eyes swept her slim torso. "Especially when my date is looking so beautiful tonight."

The casual, floor length dress that she wore was strapless and revealed her cocoa colored shoulders. Her short hair was slicked back into a wavy sculpture, complemented by dangling gold ear rings. Her makeup was perfectly applied, and the scent that she wore was a serious threat to his equilibrium.

"Well, thank you for the compliment." Dana took special care to dress for the evening. She was glad that it wasn't in vain.

Taking the exit onto the highway, she glanced at James out of the corner of her eye. He appeared to be mesmerized by the picturesque scenery.

"You've never been to Marin County before?"

James shook his head. "No, I haven't. Like I told you, the plan was to open an office in San Francisco and I planned on living there, but after being over here, I'm not too sure." He told her about Ray's offer to rent the house.

Having arrived in Sausalito, Dana maneuvered the car along the crowded streets. "So you think that you'll take it?"

"Yes, I think I might. Ray told me that his wife moved her business and her staff out here from Chicago. Her office is in San Francisco and she commutes from over here."

"Did he tell you how he flies down to L.A. several times a week to his office? Now *that's* a commute." Dana chuckled.

"I guess if he can do that, I can drive across the Golden Gate Bridge."

Dana found the restaurant where they would be dining and turned into the parking lot. Once inside, they were escorted to a table by the window that provided a spectacular view of San Francisco.

"I like this," James looked around with approval at the charming ambiance of the dimly lit interior. A jazz trio provided background music. "I haven't seen a live band in a restaurant since I don't know when." He returned his attention to Dana. "You have exquisite taste, Mrs. Mansfield."

She was glad that he was pleased. "Actually, I can't take credit for this. Bev and Ray introduced me to this place and I fell in love with it."

They ordered their meals and then settled back to await its arrival. Dana looked at James across the candle lit table, appreciating what a ruggedly handsome man he was. His golden skin glowed with health, and she really liked the bald look, although, initially, she wasn't crazy about the pierced ear. But, Sin wore an earring and made it look good. So did James, especially coupled with those bulging muscles—and of course there were those eyes. Gray eyes on a black man. How unusual.

"Are you bi-racial, James?"

Guessing the reason for the question, he gave a hearty laugh. "No, these eye balls come from a long way back, on my father's side of the family. I've been told that they come from my great, great, great, grandmother who was a slave and her master's child. My father had gray eyes too."

"Is your father living?"

"No, I lost him when I was thirteen."

"The two of you were close?"

James nodded. "As far as I was concerned, he walked on water. When he died from a heart attack my life spun out of control."

"Is that when you joined the gang?"

"Yep, and my mother was frantic. She tried everything to get me to quit. My parents were hard working people and I was their only child. They hadn't raised me to be a thug, but the gang was an outlet for all of the hurt and pain that I was feeling. Unfortunately, she didn't live to see me quit. She died when I was in jail."

"Is that her name that you have tattooed on your arm?" Dana nodded toward the artwork covered by his shirt sleeve. She looked at him expectantly.

"No." That was all that James would offer on that subject.

He turned to look out of the window making it obvious that the subject was closed. Dana didn't press.

"How did your talk with Sinclair go?"

James' head snapped around in surprise. "How did you know about that?" Sin left the house before she arrived.

"He's staying on the boat with Ray and me. When he came in I asked if he planned on talking to you while he was here, because Lord knows you two needed to talk. That's when he told me that he stopped by the house."

Since it was clear that James would be involved with their family for awhile, she hoped that the animosity between the men would be settled. His next words reassured her that might happen.

"Surprisingly, it went well. Too bad we didn't have the opportunity to talk a long time ago, a lot of things would have been settled."

Without going into detail about the encounter, he told her how they parted with a handshake. What he didn't tell her was how his talk with Sin set him free of a seething anger that had crippled him emotionally for much too long. Something else that he didn't mention to Dana was that Sinclair wanted to be an active participant in the effort to track the kidnappers.

"That's my daughter and my niece they took and I want in," he told James.

Sin indicated that he had contacts that could provide them with a decided advantage which James might need. Dismissing that possibility, James rejected the request because of the potential danger, but Sin would not be dissuaded. In the end, James made no commitment to his request, but he did promise to keep him fully informed. Sin didn't respond to that concession.

Dinner was delicious. After they finished, Dana pushed her empty plate aside and leaned across the table toward James. He could see that there was something on her mind.

"I'm glad that you and Sin soothed the waters between you because I need to tell you about something that's going to happen tomorrow." She gave him a small smile before continuing. "It seems that Sin came with me on a clandestine mission on behalf of Darnell and Thad—but, probably more Darnell, if you ask me. You see, earlier today he met with Carla and gave her a list that my niece and her husband compiled. It contained the names of twenty-five minority children from all over the country, who were abducted during the same period of time in which Nia and Gillian were taken, and these kids are still missing."

James didn't need to hear anymore. "Let me guess. As their spokesperson, Carla is going to hold a press conference and read those names."

"You've got it, and they're offering a reward for each child that is found. They want to bring awareness to the fact that when it comes to missing children, minority children are ignored by the media.

James knew that this was true. As a cop he had been an eyewitness to the media's disinterest. Blonde hair and blue eyes were the priority. If Darnell Cameron and Thad Stewart weren't major celebrities there was no doubt that public interest in the abduction of their loved ones would have waned by now.

"Sin volunteered to bring the list and the statement to Carla." Dana raised an eyebrow. "And I suspect that he had other motives for coming with me, like talking to you.

"Other than that he could have sent the list electronically, just like you could have done with the contract," James teased.

Dana gave a guilty smirk. "Okay, I'm busted, but I don't think they wanted the rest of the family to know what was going to happen. There are some members who feel the first statement issued brought unnecessary publicity.

Lord knows they don't want to generate any more, and this definitely will. But Darnell is a stubborn one."

"There's no doubt about that. Has your niece always been a rebel?"

"She sure has."

James grinned as he recalled the exploits that he had read about the superstar over the years. She lived life on her own terms. Notoriously private, she shunned Hollywood and stated publicly that walking the red carpet at award ceremonies was a waste of exercise. She gave very few interviews, and when she did grant them, she let it be known that she expected intelligent questions.

Thad Stewart was the polar opposite. He was outgoing with the public and with the media. Known as a notorious playboy, every actress, model and heiress in the country had tried to tame him, but it was the contentious diva who won his heart. When Thad and Darnell married the entire entertainment community was shocked.

"Darnell Cameron is my kind of woman," said James.

Dana folded her hands under her chin. "Oh, is she?"

James mimicked Dana's actions. "Yes, she is." He flashed a dazzling smile. "And so is her aunt."

Dana's throaty laugh shot straight to James' groin. It was as sexy as hell. This woman could prove to be a major distraction for any man.

"What are you thinking, Mr. Starr?"

"About you of course," James answered honestly. He was enjoying their flirtatious banter. "And about why I didn't know more about you."

"Why would you?"

"We had a mutual acquaintance."

"Really?   Other than Ray?   Who?"   Dana mentally reviewed the list of friends they might have in common and couldn't think of anyone. His answer surprised her.

"Mitchell Clayton, your late fiancé. I met him years ago in New York, through Ray. The three of us played golf together. Through the years he would call me when he came to New York and we'd get in some rounds of golf. I'm surprised Ray didn't tell you that I knew Mitch."

"Mitch hasn't been a topic of discussion between us in a long time," Dana admitted. The relationship with her late fiancée had not been a good one.

The shift in her mood made James sorry he brought the subject up.   As far as he could remember Mitch only mentioned Dana Mansfield once.   It was James' understanding that the couple had been engaged for years. How the man could have resisted raving about a woman like this was beyond him. Her next words startled him out of his contemplation.

"Have you ever been in love, James?" Dana's tone was somber.   "Have you ever been wounded by a relationship?" She was more than aware of the battle scars she carried.

James sighed.   The conversation was going in a direction that he'd rather not travel, but he answered honestly.

"I was in love with my girlfriend and I loved our son, but I lost them both. It's his nickname that I have tattooed on my arm."

"I'm so sorry." Dana's heart went out to him. "What happened?"

"They were murdered."   Those words brought the usual stab of pain.

Dana was shocked by his admission and curious about the details, but she refrained from asking further questions. Reaching across the table, she and placed her hand atop his. James cleared his throat to keep his emotions in check. He threaded their fingers.

"I was married when I was in the Marines, but that didn't last. It was good that we didn't have kids. That helped us make a clean break. We really weren't good for one another"

"I've been married twice." Dana sighed sadly. "It seems that when it comes to finding a good man I haven't been very lucky."

James' eyes twinkled. "Oh, I don't know. Maybe your luck will change."

Dana hoped he was right. Who knew? Maybe Lady Luck might be right around the corner for them both.

****

Under the cover of night, a dark clad figure moved effortlessly across the yard of a small house in Inglewood. His body wasn't as lithe as it used to be when he was younger, but there was still grace in his movements. Reaching the back door he removed a penlight from the small cache of tools that he carried with him. The lock on the security door wasn't as good as he thought it would be. Picking it took less than a minute. He wanted to laugh aloud at how easy it was. The lock on the door beyond turned out to be an even bigger joke.

As he stood in the darkened kitchen getting his bearings, he listened for any sounds, all the while wondering how the house's occupant could have ignored the obvious when securing his home. A dog would have been a more effective security measure than both of the locked doors. Having breached the pathetic attempt at home security, he was inside the house and now had all of the time in the world to execute his plan. By the time he left here he would know if he had been wasting his time on a wild goose chase, or if he had hit the jackpot.

CHAPTER 14

"What have I done?" Dana thought as she covered her face with her hands.

It was early morning and she was lying in bed next to James Starr. Her body was still humming from their fervent love making, an evening of passion she wouldn't easily forget. Still, she hadn't 'meant for their time together to end up like this.

James lay beside her sheet draped figure with his head propped on his hand. When Dana took a peek at him over her shoulder, she found his eyes waiting.

"Don't even try to give me that this-wasn't-supposed-to-happen line," he warned. "We're two mature adults, with three marriages between us. We're way past making excuses for our actions."

Dana couldn't deny that. Making love to James was something that had been on her mind since their many conversations over the telephone late into the night. Their latent desire for each other intensified in every word spoken. But, she hadn't expected those desires to turn into reality so soon.

James placed a kiss in her hair. "Regrets between us are useless," he murmured. "The deed is done. Anyway, you're a class act, lady, and I don't think that you're the type of woman who engages in one night stands. I know I'm not that type of man."

"I certainly hope not." Dana's body warmed at his touch. "Still, I've got to think about this." She drew away from him, but James' roaming hands wouldn't cooperate.

"We both have a lot to think about." His fingertips mapped the length of her spine.

Dana remembered how those fingers dallied with such expertise between her parted thighs only a short while ago. The sweetest of nectar was beginning to flow at the mere thought of what James was capable of doing. Once again, she tried to draw away. .

"I feel cheap going to bed with a man I hardly know," she confessed. "I've been celibate for years. Maybe that's why I was so vulnerable tonight."

"Then I'm flattered that you chose me as the one to break the drought," James whispered, placing a heated kiss between her shoulder blades that singed her bare skin. "And I don't think that you're cheap at all."

"That's good to hear."

"Then what's bothering you? Did I misinterpret what we just shared?"

"No, that didn't bother me at all."

How could it? When his mouth devoured her inner core, the spasms of pleasure rippling through her body left her withering helplessly.

"Then what is it?" A single fingertip caressed the curve of her hip.

Dana closed her eyes enjoying the sensations that his touch was causing. She needed to stop this. She turned to face him and the sheet fell from her upper torso exposing her naked breasts. James' eyes darkened with passion, but what he saw in her eyes was distress. This time, he drew away.

"Unless you're one hell of an actress, what we shared last night tells me that you care for me."

"Yes, I do. I like you a lot."

"And the feeling is mutual."

Dana propped her head on her hand and looked into his compelling eyes. "But where can this lead? I live in L.A. and you'll be up here in the Bay Area."

"You're getting ahead of yourself. Right now we're in the getting to know you stage. I say let's take it one day at a time. Besides, I happen to know that Ray and your sister had a long distance relationship before they got married. That worked out fine for them."

There was no denying that. Added to that was the fact that Bev was ten years older than Ray, and they managed to forge a love match that worked. Dana wanted what they had, but she had doubts that would happen.

"I can't give my heart away again and have it broken into pieces. It may not mend the next time."

"I understand. I feel the same way, but I'm willing to risk the possibility that mine may stay intact this time." He tweaked a dark nipple. Dana jumped in response and pushed his hand away.

"Stop that!"

James grinned. "Are you sure?" He gave the other nipple a quick flick with the tip of his tongue.

"You're not playing fair," Dana gasped. "But, I agree that we should take this slow."

"Sounds good." James lowered her to the mattress. "But right now, I want you to concentrate on us. Forget everything else except how we feel when we're together."

Dana's breath quickened. "I can do that."

His scorching tongue circled her navel. The heat radiated from his body to hers. Dana caressed his bulging biceps. *Yes, she could easily do that.*

Parting her legs gently James hovered above her. "I'm not the type of man who gives himself easily to a woman, but there is something about you that I find hard to resist."

Inserting a finger, he found her wet and ready. With practiced agility, he stroked her, alternating his efforts with his skillful tongue. The glowing embers grew hot, and then hotter until Dana ignited.

Watching the orgasm claim her, James' gray eyes glowed like a cat's in the dark. When she was able to speak, Dana paid him tribute.

"You're amazing."

James gave a dip of his head. "I'm glad that you liked it, but if you enjoyed that you're going to love this."

Retrieving a condom from the nightstand, he handed it to her. Tearing the foil off she rolled it onto his manhood with such dexterity that his hardened member came close to release. James kissed her long and hard, as a reward for being so potently thorough. Combing his fingers tenderly through the curly triangle at the entrance of her womanhood, he entered her.

He was a large man in every way and Dana's body reveled at the sensation of him inside of her. Her eyes drifted shut.

"Look at me," he asked gently.

Dana complied, having learned quickly that James liked to share the intimacy of love making. He cared that her pleasure equaled his own.

He suckled as he thrust. She moaned her delight.

"Do you like that?"

Dana's reply was loud and clear. "Oh, Yes!"

James established a rhythm that was sure to satisfy. Wrapping her legs tightly around his body, she allowed the deepest of access and James took her for a thrill ride. When they reached their destination they both exploded. Their shouts of mutual pleasure rattled the still air.

****

"She's grown," Sin informed Ray after noticing him glancing out of the houseboat window for the twentieth time. They were in the kitchen eating breakfast on the luxurious houseboat owned by Ray and his wife.

"I'm aware of that, and I'm sure that she knows what she's doing." Ray didn't sound too convincing. "But the least she could have done was call last night and tell me that she wasn't coming home."

Earlier that morning they discovered that Dana wasn't on the boat, and hadn't slept in her bed. Sin took a sip of his juice.

"Why are you so concerned? You know the man better than I do."

"True, but it does seems that you and James have a history."

"We do, but it's like I told you, we talked. I think we're cool now."

Ray nodded. He was glad that whatever was causing the animosity between the two men had been settled.

"I like James, but I don't know about him messing with my sister-in-law."

"I don't think that he would hurt her." Sin was surprised at his own words. He never had a positive thought about Starr before.

"No, not physically, but Dana is vulnerable emotionally. She's been hurt a lot in her love life and I don't think that she could take any more heartache."

After his talk with Starr, Sin wondered if his former nemesis could take any more either. James hadn't tried to hide the pain that he still carried over the death of his loved ones.

"There aren't too many people in life who haven't been hurt," Sin ventured, "and since he's human I'm sure that the same can be said for him. Maybe if the two of them get together they could heal each other's pain."

"You've got a point."

They resumed eating their meals, until Sin broke the silence.

"What do you think is going to happen with that statement that Darnell and Thad issued?" Earlier, they watched the news coverage of Carla reading the list of lost children.

Ray was honest. "As an agent, I've been involved with the media for years. First, the news pundits will make some defensive denials about the kids having been ignored. After that, they'll rush to pretend that they are interested in finding them. They might spotlight one, maybe two of them for a few weeks, until the furor dies down, and then it would be back to business as usual. *But*, with the rewards being offered, the public will have a field day dragging kids into police stations trying to claim the money, so the fake interest might go on for a little longer. Who knows, some of the kids might actually be found. It was clever of Darnell and Thad to add that monetary incentive. It might help."

Sin wanted to rail against his assessment, but sadly, Ray was right. He could only be grateful that his daughter and niece hadn't been among those children who were routinely ignored.

He was about to share that thought with Ray when the sight of Dana clamoring up the gangplank caught his attention. Ray saw her too.

"Looks like she's back."

Leaving the kitchen, they went outside to meet her and noticed that Dana was walking fast. James was behind her.

"Something's up," Sin noted her drawn eyebrows and pursed lips. "And it doesn't look good."

CHAPTER 15

Mrs. Mansfield,
I know that you're the agent for Darnell Cameron and that you are her aunt too. That's why you was picked. I want to turn myself in to you for kidnapping her daughter and that other little girl. I'll only turn myself in to you because you family and I think the police will kill me. Don't bring them or I will kill myself.

The note that Dana handed Sin was encased in a plastic sandwich bag, courtesy of James Starr. It was signed with the name Andy Vega. Beneath his name was written a P.S. that read:

Look for Jack Spencer too. I'll tell you more when I see you.

Sin looked up from the note. "Okay, he knows the name of the guy the FBI is holding? So does everybody else in the free world."

Dana nodded. "I know, but…"

"But that means that this is some sort of hoax." Ray was skeptical. "There's got to be a million kooks out there who have confessed to this."

He was right. The crazies were having a field day confessing to the kidnapping. Some people had even turned in their neighbors. Authorities in L.A. and on the Peninsula were working overtime following all of the false leads.

"What's so special about this one?" Sin wondered. He was the one who delivered the letter to Dana in the first place.

After their meeting, Carla told Sin that she had inadvertently picked out a dozen unopened letters which were examples of the many supportive ones were coming to her office since the kidnapping was revealed. She had read many of them and she thought that Dana and the families should see a few. Carla had given Sin a small bundle of letters addressed to both families, and a few addressed to Dana. Sin remembered to give Dana her correspondence before she left on her date with James. Absentmindedly, Dana slipped them inside her purse. It was while she was at James' place that she recalled having them and read the letter that she was sharing with Sin and Ray.

"You could be right about the letter being a hoax," James told Ray. "But look at the date on the envelope."

Ray complied and then expelled a long breath. "It was written two days before Jack Spencer was hauled in for questioning."

"Precisely!" It was the date that caught James' attention when Dana showed him the letter. "I've got a feeling that this is no joke."

"So we take this to the FBI," said Ray.

His statement was met with silence. Dana and James avoided eye contact with him, and Ray got the message. He looked at them in astonishment.

"I *know* that you agree with me! We've got to call Agent Conway."

James spoke up. "I think that this Vega dude is worth checking out first," It was Dana who convinced him.

After discovering the letter's contents, she was ready to fly straight to Los Angeles to confront the man. There was nothing that James could say to dissuade her, even his threat to call the authorities. She whirled on him.

"Go ahead and call them. I'm going anyway."

Grabbing her car keys, Dana headed for the door. James stopped her.

"This is not a job for amateurs," he admonished. "If this guy really is involved, it's up to the authorities to take him in."

Dana jerked away from him "I don't doubt that, but if he's not involved then they've wasted a lot of time." She took a step back. "As a matter of fact it's you who needs to go and see about this. You just signed a contract to track down all leads. I shouldn't be the one headed to Los Angeles. It should be you."

James agreed to fly to L.A. and check out Vega. If the man turned out to be a crackpot, he would be written off as another nut.

"I'm flying down there too." Dana told him. When James bristled, she quickly added, "After all I do live in Los Angeles. My Uncle Gerald is flying back here today and he can fly us both down there in no time."

That was the plan. James would follow up on the lead, and after speaking to Vega, he'd report his findings to her.

As they drove to the houseboat Dana asked him, "Are you packing?"

James laughed. "You've been watching too many detective shows." Actually, he was carrying a gun, but it was better that she didn't know that.

However, gun or no gun, Ray Wilson was adamantly against pursuing Vega.

"Have you people gone out of your minds? A federal offense has been committed!. This…this note," he slapped it with his hand, "may be evidence. You can't go looking for this person on your own."

"That's exactly what James' agency is being paid to do!" Dana countered.

Her brother-in-law turned to Sin. "Man, I know you can't agree with this. Talk to these people."

"There's only one thing for me to say," Sin said quietly. He turned to James. "If this man had anything to do with taking my daughter and my niece, I want to be there when you talk to him."

"What?" Ray was flabbergasted. "Am I the only sane one on this boat?"

Sin and James ignored him. Their eyes locked.

"I told you the deal," Sin reminded him. "Anyway, I've got the address and I know his name. I'll go after him with or without you."

James had no doubt that he would. Their encounter yesterday confirmed that despite Sin's urbane polish, there was still plenty of street in him. He could handle himself. James had the feeling that if anything did go down, Sin just might be the one who would have his back. Still, he resisted.

"My agency has employees in L.A. If I need someone to go with me, it will be one of them."

"You've got to pay them on what might be a long shot," Sin reminded him. "I come free."

"This is business. I'm not going to be responsible for a civilian."

"Dana, write up a document releasing Starr of any responsibility for my safety and I'll sign it," said Sin.

Dana agreed, "Will do."

"Oh hell no!" Ray lamented. "I'm calling Agent Conway."

Reaching into his jacket, Ray withdrew his cell phone. Sin removed it from his hand so smoothly that for a second Ray didn't know that it was gone.

"Don't be silly, Ray. It's my decision, and I'm going."

Dana's tone was harsh. "If you don't want to go along with this, get on the plane and fly back to Stillwaters, but don't interfere."

"I've been doing this for quite some time," James assured Ray. "I know what I'm doing. If this guy is one of the abductors, then, believe me, the cops will be called."

His words made Ray feel a bit better, but not much. "You're not going with him to talk to this man, are you Dana?"

"No, she's not," James interjected firmly. "I told her I'd call her as soon as I know what's up."

Dana gave James a side eye before turning her attention to Ray. "Either go along, or go away. We don't have any more time to waste on this."

Ray watched as the trio walked away, ready to make plans to leave for Los Angeles. Uttering an expletive, he followed them, reluctantly, hoping against hope that he wasn't making a big mistake.

****

James pulled the car in front of the box-like house and parked. It was late morning and they had wasted no time getting here. Graciously, Dana's uncle changed his plans and flew them to Los Angeles. They didn't share the reason for the trip. Dana simply informed him that it was important.

The plan was for James and Sin to drive to the house and question the man calling himself Andy Vega. In the beginning, Dana hadn't been in that plan, but when they arrived in L.A. it was clear that she had her own agenda.

She insisted that she was going to the house with them. James t felt that it might be dangerous, but Dana's counterargument was effective.

"Andy Vega asked to see me. I doubt if he'll open his door to two men without me being with you."

No one could argue with that, and when Dana was included on the trip to the Vega house, Ray changed his mind about waiting in his L.A. office for a call to recount the visit's outcome. He decided to go to with them.

"Bev would never forgive me if I let something happen to you," he told Dana.

Nobody said it, but the others were wondering how he was going to protect her. Ray wondered too. Unlike James and Sin, he had no street cred, but at least he would be there to help in any way he could.

Having arrived at their destination, Dana looked out of the window at the house, with its peeling paint, missing roof shingles and cracked porch steps. The neighborhood in which it was located was rife with homes that were vacant or in need of repair. Spiked fences, security doors and barred windows were the norm. The lawn in front of this particular house was more dirt than grass. Nothing about the place was inviting.

"This ought to be good," she drawled.

"I feel you," Sin agreed from the back seat. He flexed the leg that held the ankle holster containing his weapon. He hoped that he wouldn't have to use it; but if this man was one of the abductors, he just might put the weapon to good use. "Are you ready?" he asked Dana.

She nodded and turned to James. "Are you?"

"As ready as I'll ever be."

Sliding out of the car, he rounded it and opened the door for a determined looking Dana. She was ready to confront this man, whoever he was, and James was proud of her. Behind the sophisticated veneer and power suits was a woman who was tougher than she looked.

James, Dana and Sin crossed the street toward the house. Ray opted to stay in the car as an unofficial lookout. They had decided that three men accompanying Dana to the front door might look like overkill. It was going to be hard enough convincing Vega that James and Sin weren't cops.

Slouching down in the back seat, Ray felt uncomfortable in this neighborhood. It was a long way from Beverly Hills. The irony was that he grew up in a working class area of Detroit much like this one. Of course, the homes weren't dilapidated or vacant, and there were no bars on the windows and doors. Plus, in his old neighborhood signs of life were everywhere.

There wasn't a sound around here, no voices, no laughter, not even the twitter of birds in the trees. No people walked the streets. It was eerie. That's why when he heard the quiet hum of an automobile engine he sat up. Glancing over his shoulder he saw an unassuming mid-size sedan slowly moving down the street. It was occupied by one person, a man. As the car passed, Ray saw the man glance at the trio, who now stood on the crumbling stoop knocking on the security door of Vega's house. The driver turned to look into the car in which Ray was sitting. For a split second their eyes met and then the car continued down the street. Ray watched it turn a corner and disappear.

His brows knitted. There was something familiar about the man in that car. It wasn't anything that he could discern in the brief glimpse that he had of him, still— Ray slouched back down in his seat.

At the front door Dana got no response to her knock. She turned to James.

"Maybe he saw us walking up to the door and thinks that you and Sin are cops."

"Call his name," James suggested.

Knocking harder, Dana called out to him. "Mr. Vega? It's Dana Mansfield. You wrote and asked me to come see you. I'm here with two friends of mine. They're not the police."

She knocked again. There was still no answer.

"I'll try around the back," Sin suggested.

James nodded. Dana continued knocking. Sin followed the weed strewn path that led to the back of the house, stopping, momentarily, to retrieve his gun. Concealing it in his pocket, he stepped cautiously into the backyard.

It was as ill-kept as the front of the house, with trash and other miscellaneous items scattered in the sparse patches of grass. A high, wooden fence with missing planks enclosed the yard.

Approaching the back door, Sin stood for a moment listening. He couldn't detect a sound inside the house. He knocked on the security door, taking care not to call out. Andy was expecting Dana, a male voice might spook him.

There was no answer to his knock. Either AndyVega wasn't going to answer, or there was no one home.

When they approached the house, Sin had observed that the house on the right of this one appeared to be occupied. A car was parked in front of it. The house on the left was boarded up, apparently abandoned.

Since there was no response to his knock, Sin decided that he would approach the neighbor and see if he could get some information about this Andy character. Turning to leave, he inadvertently gave the handle of the security door a slight tug. To his surprise, it opened.

CHAPTER 16

Ray watched as Dana and James went around the side of the house where Sin had disappeared earlier. The neighborhood was beginning to come alive, and Ray was ready to go. A man and woman next door to Vega's house came out of their home, got into their car and drove away. They seemed mildly curious about Ray sitting in the car across the street, but didn't acknowledge his presence as they drove by. A short while later a teenage boy came out of the same house. He walked in the opposite direction and never looked at the car parked across the street—so much for curious neighbors.

The car Ray was sitting in was parked in front of an empty lot that once held a home. The crumbled front steps were still visible among the weeds and trash. Another empty lot was next to that one. There wasn't another occupied house until two lots down. Observing Vega's house, Ray could clearly see that in this neighborhood privacy wasn't an issue.

It was then that he noticed Dana rushing back around the front of the house. The look of horror on her face propelled Ray out of the car and across the street. She met him at the sidewalk and threw herself into his arms.

"He's dead!" Dana shrieked.

Loosening his grip on her, Ray took a step back, holding her at arm's length.

"What are you talking about? Who's dead?"

"In there!" She pointed a shaky finger toward the house just as James came rushing around the side yard. He was on his cell phone. His expression was grim. Fear gripped Ray.

"What happened?"

Putting his phone away, James folded a still trembling Dana in his arms before addressing Ray.

"Somebody beat and tortured the guy inside the house. If that's Andy Vega in there it doesn't look good."

Stunned, Ray's jaw dropped. "Dana said that he was dead."

"Close to it," James tightened his hold on Dana. "I called 9-1-1. An ambulance is on the way."

"You mean he's alive?" Dana sounded hopeful.

James nodded. "Sin's with him. I came out to see about you."

Still uncertain about what was happening; Ray took a fortified breath and decided to see for himself. He started walking to the house, heading around the side yard.

"Don't touch anything," James called out to him. He took a thin pair of plastic gloves from his jacket pocket. "Use these." He ordered with no further explanation. Ray took them from him.

Entering the opened back door, Ray found it was dim inside the house. The only light emitted was filtering through the closed kitchen curtains. Inside appeared to be smaller than the outside. The place was hot, stuffy and smelled like fried grease. Ray's stomach roiled. The distance between the kitchen and the cluttered living room was only a few steps.

"Sinclair?" he called cautiously. There was no sign of him.

"In here," a voice called to Ray.

He followed the sound, turning into a short hallway. Straight ahead was a bedroom with an unmade bed that looked as though it was blocking the doorway. Immediately to his right was a bathroom, where Sin stood, rifling through the medicine cabinet. He wore a pair of thin plastic gloves like the ones that James had given Ray.

"What's going on?' The bathroom was filthy, and smelled like urine.

Sin gestured toward the bathtub with his thumb. Ray glanced in that direction and gasped. Propped up in the tub was a dark haired man. His eyes were blindfolded, his mouth was agape, and his face was bruised and battered.

"What happened?" Ray's voice was strangled. He couldn't believe what he was seeing.

Sin gave a nonchalant shrug. "From the look of it somebody beat him to a bloody pulp and added a little water torture for good measure." He read the name on the prescription bottle that he took from the medicine cabinet. "Andy Vega."

"He looks like he's dead." Ray could hardly breathe. What the hell was going on?

"He was barely breathing when we found him," Sin said seemingly unfazed by the carnage. "Do you have a writing pen on you?"

Ray was taken aback by his attitude. "No I don't!" "Man! There's a body in the bathtub and you're acting like it's an everyday thing! Aren't you concerned?"

Sin's demeanor didn't change. "If this man put his hands on those girls, then no, I don't give a damn if he lives or dies. He better be glad that I didn't get to him first." He slipped the prescription bottle into his pants pocket.

Ray was beside himself. "Are you crazy? You're taking evidence from the man's house. That's a criminal offense!"

"Hey, all I did was ask you for a pen to write something down." Sin slammed the door to the cabinet shut.

"Hell! I'm out of here. I'm not losing my law license over this." Ray backed out of the doorway and bumped into James.

"Find anything?" James asked Sin, peering over Ray's shoulder.

"A prescription with his name and his doctor's name on it," Sin withdrew the bottle from his pocket to show him.

"And please give him a pen and hope that we don't all go to jail," Ray barked as he moved past James. "I'll see you two outside."

Ray hurried out of the room, while James tossed Sin a writing pen. Sin tore a paper towel from a nearby roll and began scribbling the information he needed.

"How's Dana doing?"

"She's still shaken. I asked her to take a seat in front and wait for the ambulance I called to help him."

It was Sin who discovered the bloodied man in the tub. When James and Dana joined him, James tried to shield her from the shocking sight, but was unsuccessful. He muffled her screams in his chest. Sin walked her to the back door and sent her outside. He returned to the bathroom to find James checking the man for signs of life.

"Have you checked his pulse again?" James looked pass Sin to the unconscious victim.

"No." Sin kept writing. It was obvious that he wasn't interested in doing so.

"When you checked the house, did you find anything in his bedroom?"

"No, I could hardly find the bed. The man is a pig." Sin handed the pen back to James, and then squeezed by him and exited the tiny space.

"You three had better get out of here," James advised as he checked on the man.

Sin needed no further explanation. He left the house and joined Dana and Ray outside. Dana was seated on the stoop massaging her temples. Looking distressed, Ray was pacing up and down the sidewalk. Sin surveyed the empty street before calling out to Ray.

"Hey, man! We've got to go."

Ray hurried to join them. Dana looked up at Sin

"Go where?"

"If we don't want to be involved in any publicity about this thing we've got to leave before help arrives." Sin pulled the gloves from his hands and stuffed them in his pocket.

Ray agreed. "I know I don't want to be involved in this. Let's walk around the corner and call a cab to pick us up while we still have time."

Dana wasn't sure. "What about James?"

"Starr will be okay." Sin reached down to help a still shaken Dana up from the step. "He was hired to track these guys down, so he's got a legitimate excuse for being here. We don't."

He started walking out of the yard toward the sidewalk. Ray followed, but Dana resisted.

"What about that poor man. Is he still alive?"

"I don't know. James is checking." Sin gently prodded her to the street. They walked casually, aware that dressed in their expensive, designer clothes they stood out in what was left of this decaying neighborhood.

The sound of a siren in the distance hurried their steps as they put distance between them and the Vega house.

"Maybe that's the ambulance." As long as Dana lived she would never forget the battered face of the man in the bathtub.

"I doubt it," Sin said dryly. "We'll probably be in the cab and half way across town by the time the cops or the ambulance gets here. Unfortunately, these kinds of neighborhoods don't usually get quick responses."

Dana observed Sin. She and Ray were both nervous wrecks, but Sin appeared to be more frustrated than anxious.

"Are you disappointed because we didn't get to Andy before somebody else did?" she asked.

"Actually I was just thinking. I figure that it took at least three of them, maybe four, to carry the kidnapping off. If Vega dies, we lose an important piece of the puzzle, but I'm conflicted about whether I want him dead or alive."

Both Dana and Ray understood what he meant. She wondered aloud.

"Who could do something like this?"

"It was probably one of his cohorts," Sin speculated. "I guess what they say is true. There's no honor among thieves."

****

Entering his hotel room, Hardman was still berating himself for having made the foolish mistake of driving pass Vega's house. He slipped out of the place successfully, and hiked to his rental car without encountering anyone on the street.

When he retrieved the car, he should have taken the opposite route out of the neighborhood, but for some reason, that made no sense, he chose to pass the house. It came as a surprise to see the trio standing at the front door. He wondered about them, as well as the man sitting in the parked car. It was obvious that they didn't belong in the neighborhood. Were they LAPD or FBI? Had the authorities tracked down the second kidnapper so soon? He doubted it. His glimpse at the visitors was brief, but they didn't look as if they were law officers, and the man sitting in the car appeared wary.

Whoever they were, they could knock on the door forever. They'd never get a response. The guy who told him that his name was Andy Vega would not be responding. He wasn't dead when Hardman left, but he should be by now.

Shedding his clothes, Hardman stepped into the shower to wash off the grime of his night's work. After drying off, he felt refreshed.

While the rest of L.A. readied itself for the day, he climbed between the sheets to sleep, but his mind wandered back to the events of last night. It had all been too easy.

Once inside the tiny house, he stole silently into the bedroom where his prey was sleeping. Once Vega was overpowered, Hardman applied a blindfold and a gag. Dragging him to the bathtub, he proceeded to beat the information he needed out of him. The man proved to be tougher than he looked because it took a while. It wasn't until he applied a water torture technique he learned in his earlier life, that he got the information he wanted—two names.

One was Jack Spencer. Andy told him that he was the "person of interest" who was being held by the authorities. Hardman had no faith in the system. He could only hope that the authorities didn't blow that one.

The second name Andy gave him was described as the man who orchestrated every step of the failed kidnapping— a misadventure thwarted by the iron-clad will of one little girl, Gillian Reasoner.

That thought brought a smile to Hardman's face. The kid had spunk. He liked that.

Tomorrow he would plan his move regarding the second man who was to be his next target. After a good sleep, it might become clear how he would settle that score.

CHAPTER 17

"The media hasn't given up and neither has the paparazzi. They're still hanging around the office as well as your new condo," Dana's administrative assistant called to warn her.

Forewarned, Dana decided to avoid both places. After the taxi Ray called picked the three of them up not far from the house they fled, Dana directed the driver to take her to a Come Right Inn owned by her cousin. The luxury bed and breakfast was nestled in the canyons of L.A. and offered the comfort and privacy that she needed. Sin decided to check into the Inn too. Despite the media scrutiny, Ray decided to go to his Beverly Hills office. All three of them waited to hear from James regarding Andy Vega.

Relaxing in her luxurious room, Dana thought about James and the intimacy they shared less than 24 hours ago. He was such a gentle, considerate lover. Yet, that hadn't come as a surprise. For reasons she couldn't explain, she expected that from him. She really liked the man, but she doubted that their attraction to each other would go any further. She wasn't being dramatic when she told him that she didn't want to take the chance on having another failed relationship.

A knock on the room door interrupted her thoughts. When she opened the door, Sin stood on the other side.

"I've got an update from Stillwaters," he said as he walked into the room. She directed him to a wing-back chair, settling in the one opposite him.

"I just got off the phone with Nedra. She said to tell you hello, and that the girls are doing fine, especially Gillian. She's still in her queen bee mode."

"Nothing new about that," Dana chuckled.

"I filled Nedra, Darnell and Thad in on the second suspect and what happened."

"I called Bev to tell her, but Ray had already spoken to her. Have you heard anything from Agent Conway?"

"No, I haven't." Sin ran a hand over his tired eyes. "I'm going to wait until we hear from Starr." He noticed how Dana avoided his eyes when he mentioned James Starr. For a moment there was an uncomfortable silence.

"I'm not one to judge," he told her quietly.

Dana's eyes slid to his. "I didn't think that you were, but I know that James and you aren't the best of friends."

"That has nothing to do with your relationship with him…"

"No, no, no," Dana denied vehemently. "There's no relationship. We just enjoy each other's company."

Sin shrugged. "I stand corrected."

"Speaking of James, I noticed how you and he were like some kind of commando squad when we were inside the house.

When Vega's battered body was discovered in the tub, James whipped out a gun, and, to Dana's surprise, so did Sin.

"I didn't know that you carried a weapon." Dana wasn't sure what to think about that bit of information.

Sin gave her a knowing smile. "And I noticed that you didn't tell Ray about that."

"Hey, I'm not going to complain about two men who can take care of business."

He laughed at her retort, glad that she didn't question him further about the gun he was carrying. He gave her a nod of approval.

"You're all right with me, Dana."

Thinking back to when he first met her, Sin thought of Dana as flighty and self-centered in her personal life, but hard as nails when it came to negotiating for her clients. However, since her accident, a few years ago, when she tumbled down a flight of stairs in her home and was seriously injured, she seemed to have mellowed. She was much more caring and considerate than in the past.

Dana's cell phone rang. James was on the other end.

"Hey there," he greeted softly. "Did you have any trouble getting out of the neighborhood?"

"No, a cab eventually showed up. How did things go at the house? "And before you answer, I'm putting you on speaker phone because Sin is here." Instantly, James became all business.

"The guy was going into cardiac arrest by the time the ambulance arrived," James told them. "I was giving him mouth-to-mouth when they took over. I gave the cops my statement, but I didn't mention you guys."

"If they're thorough in their investigation, they'll eventually find out that we were there," said Sin. "We stuck out like sore thumbs walking through that neighborhood. The cabbie that picked us up asked if we were lost tourists."

"We need to contact the authorities and tell them we were there and why we left," Dana concluded. "I doubt if we'll be charged with anything, but it could get messy if they find out we left."

Sin nodded. "I agree."

James informed them that he was at the hospital. "Vega is in intensive care. They're not sure if he's going to make it. If he does they think that he'll be a vegetable."

"He was beaten that viciously?" Dana couldn't help but feel for the man.

"It was pretty bad. According to the doctor there's a lot of trauma."

Sin didn't waste any sympathy. "My heart bleeds." He rose. "I'm going to call Nedra."

Excusing himself, Sin left the room. Dana and James were left alone to talk. His voice softened.

"I'm aware that the whole scene in that house was hard on you, and what I really want to know is how you're doing?"

Dana was touched by his sensitivity. "I'll probably have nightmares for a while, so I'd rather not think about it."

"Maybe I can help ease those nightmares," James hinted.

"I'm sure there's something you could do," she returned suggestively.

"I've got one more stop to make and then I'll come by and we'll see what happens. Where are you, at your office?"

"No, I'm still dodging the media. I'm staying at my cousin's Come Right Inn." She gave him the address and her room number. "I'll be waiting."

****

"So you contacted me after the fact?" Agent Conway glared at James through narrowed eyes as he fingered the plastic encased letter addressed to Dana.

James didn't react to his censure. "The family has hired our agency to investigate and I was only doing my job."

"No, you were interfering with an ongoing investigation!" The agent's voice rose in frustration. "I could arrest you for that."

James remained unfazed. "You could, but I've given you the evidence. I did my best to make sure that it wasn't contaminated. I called the authorities when I found the victim. I even tried to save his life. What else is a citizen to do?"

The agent stared at James suspiciously, but James held his gaze. He could understand how the man felt. As an officer of the law he was under tremendous pressure to find the people responsible for the kidnapping. The public wanted arrests and a quick resolution, like on TV or in the movies. Conway was the lead investigator. A successful end to this case was on his shoulders, and the load was heavy. Mistakes were unacceptable.

"I'm here to help, not to hinder," James told him empathizing with his plight. "After all, we're working for the same cause. I can't afford to make mistakes either."

"But you can make yours in private."

James was surprised at the man's candor. "I could have kept the letter to myself. I could have walked away from that house and you might not have known that I was even there. Instead, I brought this letter to your office. I'm not the enemy. This case is just as important to us as it is to you. It's a big one for our security firm. My partner and I are handling it personally. He's flying in later today to see what he can do to help me."

"Oh, great! I'll have two of you roaming around L.A. and getting in the way." It was clear that Agent Conway didn't relish the prospect.

James didn't care one way or the other how Conway felt. He was hired to do a job, and he was going to do it.

James stood, ready to leave the agent's office. "How's the interrogation of Jack Spencer going?"

"Fine," Conway replied curtly. He turned to his computer screen in dismissal.

James knew that any information that he might glean from this agent would be nonexistent. It was clear that Conway resented him. He saw James' agency as competition. His intention was to shut them out.

James closed the door behind him. He was used to the Agent Conways in this world. No problem. He would do what he had to do.

****

"So the jobs going to be a little harder," Dana surmised after reviewing what James told her about his talk with Agent Conway.

"Maybe so, maybe not." James lay at the foot of Dana's bed playing with her toes as they talked. Her pedicure was perfect. The sizzling red polish on her toenails matched the color on her manicured fingernails. "Have I told you that you're too sexy to be believed?"

"Thanks for the compliment."

She ran her big toe slowly down his cheek. Catching her foot he planted a kiss in her instep, reigniting a slow burn.

"Have I told you that I like your style, Mr. Starr?"

"Yes you have Mrs. Mansfield, and it's appreciated."

"I try to please," Dana growled. She liked this playful side of him, especially since he seemed to be such a serious man.

After their latest workout, Dana figured that if James was as good at investigating as he was at making love, then the case should be solved very soon. She was thoroughly satisfied. Her mind was still in a fog. It took a few seconds before she realized that he was talking to her.

"What did you say?"

"I need to talk to Gillian," James repeated. "And I've got to get out to that house where the girls were kept and look around."

Using her foot to tilt his chin up to look at her, Dana frowned. "I can't believe that you're talking about business right now. After all, I am heading back to my home town tomorrow."

"I know, and I'm going to miss you."

Using his elbows, he slowly dragged his large body over Dana's naked torso, placing kisses in strategic places along the way. Placing a long, slow kiss on her lips, he reversed their positions and pulled her on top of him. Dana placed her head on his massive chest.

James gave a contented sigh. It had been a long time since he felt this good.

"I have an idea. Instead of going back to Stillwaters why don't you come to Tiburon and stay with me. I've decided to take Ray up on renting his old place. You'll have the privacy that you need there until all of this dies down."

He wanted her with him. He wanted to get to know her better. He wanted to know everything about her.

As she listened to the steady beat of his heart, Dana didn't respond at first. With James she felt protected. With him she felt safe. Being with this man could easily become a habit, but the reality was that all habits weren't good for you.

"I like the offer, but I don't think that staying together at this point would be good for either of us." She paused. "No, let me correct that. It wouldn't be good for *me*. We might be moving a little too fast."

James drew back, trying not to feel hurt by her words. After all, he was the one who suggested that they take it slow.

"I understand, but I can't help but think that we have a pretty good thing going on here."

"I think that we do too, but I've learned from past relationships that when I move too fast it turns out to be a mistake. I've been married to an abuser..."

James started. "Someone hit you?" Dana nodded.

"And I've been married to a user. It's taken me a while to admit this, but my engagement to Mitch wasn't a wise decision either."

James was aware that she might be right. On those few occasions when Mitch and he socialized, he was a witness to the fact that Mitch didn't act like a man with a fiancée.

"Listen, James, in the time that we've known each other, you've become very special to me. But you're as complex as I am. We need to get to know and understand each other's complexities if this thing is going to work."

Dana was at the stage in her life where she was no longer so desperate for affection that she was willing to go along to get along. The train had left that station. Time and experience made her demand more from a man than being a good lover. Any man who wanted to come into her life had to demonstrate both character and substance. James seemed to have both, but time would tell.

Setting Dana beside him, James scooted up in the bed. He needed to put a bit of distance between them. He was letting lust overrule logic. At some point common sense was needed.

"I can't argue with what you've said. We don't really know each other that well. There are things that do need to be said." He fell silent for a moment as he stared into space, lost in thought.

Dana missed the warmth of his embrace the moment that their bodies parted, but she forced herself to ignore the ardent need to be back in his arms. From his demeanor it appeared that there was something he wanted to share with her. He was a difficult man to read, and she wasn't sure what to expect next; but what he did say wasn't what she had expected to hear.

"I want to tell you about my son and his mother. If you want to know anything about me you need to know about them."

For the next hour Dana listened as he revealed a part of his life that she was certain he rarely talked about. Although decades had passed since he lost the two people he loved so deeply, he spoke as if they died yesterday.

James wanted Dana to know about the shield he had put around his heart. Never again did he want to feel the agony of such loss. He was letting her know that emotional involvement was as risky for him as it was for her.

After he finished talking, James felt drained. He never told anyone, other than Nate, how the death of Regina and Pookie had affected him; or how much guilt he carried because of the way they died. He certainly never told anyone about the depth of the pain that he carried. He wasn't sure what possessed him to do so this time, except that unlike the women in his past, he sensed that Dana might understand.

She felt humbled by the fact that he shared something so special with her. They lay in silence. Nothing else needed to be said.

Dana and James were sleeping soundly when the ring of a cell phone woke them both. Startled, Dana sat straight up. She looked around sleepily.

"What time is it.?"

A groggy James peered at the clock on the nightstand. "Oh damn! I don't believe it! We've been asleep for hours!" Retrieving his cell phone from the night stand, he checked caller ID. "Damn! It's Nate," he groaned. "I forgot to pick him up at the airport!"

Answering the call, he was about to apologize, when the voice on the other end caught him off guard. It wasn't his partner speaking.

"Is this James Starr?"

"Yes, it is."

Rolling out of the bed, Dana started getting dressed when an agonized moan from James caught her attention. She turned, and her heartbeat quickened at the stricken look on his face.

"What's wrong?"

Still gripping his cell phone, he looked at it and then at her. "It's a police officer. He said that Nate had a heart attack at the airport. He's dead."

CHAPTER 18

"Daddy, when can we come home?"

His daughter's plaintive inquiry was like a dagger in Sin's heart. Strangers had come out of nowhere and disrupted his family's life.

"We'll all be home together soon," he assured her with the hope that what he was saying was true. "But I thought that you loved it in Stillwaters."

"I do, but I've got to get back to school. I'm keeping up with the class, but it's not the same as being there in person. Anyway, most of the cousins have gone home now, and the ones who live here go to school in another town, so I'm by myself most of the time. I don't have anyone to play with except Nia."

Sin was livid. His baby girl was suffering. Somebody was going to pay for this! He tried to sound conciliatory.

"Well, Trevor is there with you."

He knew that really didn't matter. A fifteen year old boy keeping his twelve year old sister company would be nothing short of a miracle, as Gillian informed him.

"That's no big deal! When he's not doing school work, he's working at the grocery store or playing basketball at the Cove." Her voice softened. "I miss home, Daddy. I miss you and I miss Sweet too."

Gillian and Brandon Plaine's son, Sweet, were best friends. They were inseparable. Brandon told Sin that his son was waging a relentless campaign trying to get him to stop covering the kidnapping so that Gillian could come home. The boy blamed the media for her having to stay away.

"When all of this dies down you can come home," Sin assured his daughter. He didn't have the heart to tell her that he didn't know when that would be.

"Okay," was her sad reply.

Sin sensed that she was aware that it might take some time. "I love you," he replied.

"I'm glad to hear that." Nedra's sultry voice came to him from the other end of the line. Gillian had handed the telephone to her mother. Sin warmed at the sound of her voice.

"Hey, baby. Our little girl sounds like a bird trapped in a gilded cage."

"You can't contain the wind," Nedra said wisely, "but she'll survive. Have you heard anything else about that poor man that was found beaten in that house?"

Poor man? Sin didn't agree with that description.

"Nope, he's still in intensive care. I called the local FBI office and nobody will tell me anything about the guy they're still questioning."

"So does that mean that he's talking or not?"

"It means that whatever happened, they're not going to share it with me," he said flatly. He planned on getting around that by calling some contacts that he knew. "How is everybody in Stillwaters taking the statement that Carla released?"

Nedra sighed. "The aunts, uncles and cousins understand its importance, and are behind it. Aunt Ginny didn't like the way that it was done. She collared Darnell, Thad and me, and said that she didn't appreciate the secrecy and she knew that the whole thing was instigated by Darnell."

Sin snickered. "Yep, there's no doubt it had her fingerprints all over it."

His sister was the one who did the research on missing children and decided that minorities should be highlighted while the public's attention was on the subject of kidnapping. She brought the idea to the others, and they agreed that the matter was an important one and should be revealed. But, everyone was aware that the renewed attention could mean further delay in returning to their normal lives.

"Was your aunt very angry?" He knew that Ginny Little, the formidable leader of the Stillwaters clan, was one of the most even tempered people he knew. Yet, even she could be pushed just so far.

"She was more hurt than angry. We should have told her the plan up front."

Sin could agree with that logic, but what was done was done. His main concern was the present.

"I miss you, baby. Being away from you is killing me." His need for her was consuming him. Not only did he need the comfort of her body but the strength of her presence. She was his rock.

"I miss you too, love. You don't know how much." Her voice lowered to a mere whisper. "I ache for you."

Sin got the message. "In how many places?" he asked hotly, ready for some dirty talk.

Nedra cleared her throat. "Your daughter is lying here in bed beside me right now."

"Great." Sin drawled, trying to reel in his libido. He loved his daughter but— "Kick her to the curb."

"Shame on you," Nedra snickered. "I'll call you later and we can continue this conversation."

"Is that a promise?"

"It certainly is."

"All right, but we'll be staying in L.A. another day to see if we can get a handle on whether that dude that we found is really one of the kidnappers. After that, I'll be home. Tell our daughter not to get too comfortable because soon I'll be the one lying in bed next to you."

"I can't wait," Nedra purred.

Bidding her goodbye, he hung up before it became difficult to walk. Not only could he feel his nature rising, but his anger was rising too. He wanted his old life back!

His eldest son, Colin, was back at Stanford and the media was still hounding him for an interview. Nobody knew when Trevor and Gillian could go back to school without a hassle. Nedra and he were forced to run their businesses remotely. As for his love life, it was being interfered with on all levels. *Damn!*

He didn't like it that his wife was expressing sympathy for the "poor" man who might be responsible for the disruption in their lives. If he was guilty, Sin had no sympathy for him. There was a time in his life that death would have been the man's fate if he had gotten to him first. Sometimes he wondered if it wasn't for his wife's influence where he would be.

Nedra was his reason for living. She was the best thing that ever happened to him. It was her goodness and kindness that made him a better man. She had chipped away at the hard shell that he built around his heart as the result of being an orphan surviving alone on the streets. She helped soften his heart in so many ways. Yet, he still would have beaten Andy Vega to a pulp without a second thought if he had found that he was guilty of the kidnapping. As a matter of fact, he would kick the ass of that "person of interest" that they had in custody if given the chance.

Yes, there was goodness and kindness in him that had been demonstrated in many ways. Still, he couldn't deny that there was a dark side to his personality that he had to work hard to suppress.

As he and Darnell got to know each other better as brother and sister, he discovered that this was one of the attributes they shared. Enemies had better beware. They took no prisoners. It made him wonder if the source of such a personality trait might have come from the parent they had in common.

****

Hardman awakened slowly, slipping into consciousness gradually. He had slept hard, and was disoriented when he awakened.

Swinging his legs to the floor, he sat on the side of the bed until he could get his bearings. A glance at the clock showed that it was 6:00 in the evening. He had slept nearly an entire day.

He flexed his knuckles. They were sore from the beating he gave Vega, but they weren't bruised. He used an old trick he learned long ago to get the information that he needed from the man, a sock filled with rocks. That and a little water torture got the job done. It was good to know that some of the old ways still worked. Vega had squealed like a pig.

Hardman turned on the television and watched the local and national news. The kidnapping was still a headline story. Other than the "person of interest" remaining in custody, there was no additional information.

What dominated the news was a statement that was issued by Darnell Cameron and Thad Stewart about missing children of color.

As Hardman channel surfed, it seemed that nearly every TV news division was stumbling over itself to disprove the accusation that they racially discriminated when it came to missing persons. In the space of a few hours, reporters had scoured the country for missing minorities and were featuring them and their distraught families on air. The vignettes were familiar and tugged at the heart strings. They were also long overdue.

Hardman was proud of Darnell and her husband. They were using their celebrity to try and make a difference. What an amazing young woman Darnell turned out to be. No doubt she inherited such compassion from her mother. It certainly hadn't come from him.

He didn't like to think about Darnell's mother. It hurt too much. As for Sinclair's mother, he still didn't have a handle on that one. His only clue was that Sinclair was older than Darnell, and he knew that she was in her thirties.

The age difference meant that the liaison with Sinclair's mother must have happened when Hardman was in his teens. The reality was, before Darnell's mother there had been no woman in his life that he loved. Whoever this woman was, she had to have been a temporary dalliance.

He was snapped out of his musings by another news flash. A reporter was standing in front of an all too familiar house stating that a man had been found inside beaten nearly to death. The man was in intensive care, but the motive for the beating hadn't been determined. Robbery had not been ruled out.

Vega's name, his age and place of employment were provided and that was it. Like countless others, he was relegated to a few lines on the evening news. There was no mention of his being tied to the kidnapping. That omission put Hardman on alert.

He had been surviving too long in the underbelly of society not to be able to read between the lines when it came to the law. The authorities were holding something back. Perhaps the "person of interest" that was in custody was doing some talking. If so, Hardman had better make his move so that he could get to the next prick before the cops picked the third kidnapper up.

He headed for the bathroom to shower, feeling no sense of urgency. No one would ever know that he was the one who beat kidnapper number two. If Vega lived, he doubted if he would ever speak again. Even if he could, all Vega could tell anyone was that a masked man beat the crap out of him until he told the names of all of the people involved in the kidnapping of Nia Stewart and Gillian Reasoner.

As for the "person of interest", he was as guilty as hell. Hopefully, the law would take care of him. If that didn't happen and the man was unlucky enough to get released, then Hardman planned on tracking him down and seeing to it that he paid for what he did with his life.

Hardman stepped into the steaming hot water feeling exhilarated. It was good to know that years of self-imposed exile had not dulled his skills. They had merely been laying dormant, waiting to rise again.

CHAPTER 19

"He was only fifty-eight years old," James said sadly as he stood in the middle of Nathan Webb's office. Ray stood beside him as James looked around the orderly space that had served as his partner's second home. He couldn't count the nights that he would peek into this office and see Nate's feet propped on his desk, while he read a report or did research for a case. That would be no more. His friend, his partner, his father figure was dead.

"I'm sure he would have gone to a doctor if he knew that he had a heart defect." Ray hoped his words were consoling, but he doubted if they could be. Nate's death had left James devastated.

From the moment James received the telephone call about his partner, he had been walking around in a daze. He couldn't believe that the man who had helped get him off the streets, who had helped guide his life as a young man, who he admired more than any other was gone— suddenly and without any warning. How could it be?

James was called because his name and number were in Nate's wallet and he designated him as his next of kin. The officer used Nate's telephone to call him.

Dana went with him to the morgue to identify Nate's body. His friend's death resurrected all of the pain that James felt when Regina and Pookie died. He hadn't cried since they died, but he sat on a bench outside of the morgue and shed long forgotten tears. Dana sat beside him.

It was she who called Ray. He met them at the hospital and escorted them back to the Come Right Inn. While James made arrangements to transport Nate's body back East, Dana made arrangements to fly back with him, and Ray decided that he would go too.

He hadn't known Nathan well, but he did know James, and he could see that he needed his support. He asked Bev, to accompany him. Sin flew to Stillwaters to be with his family, and the unofficial effort to track down the kidnappers was put on temporary hold.

That was a week ago. The memorial service held yesterday for Nathan Webb had been simple and tasteful. Later today, James was scheduled to fly back to the West Coast with Dana, Ray and Bev. James had stopped by the Webb Starr office to pick up some files before leaving, and Ray volunteered to go with him.

As they moved through the office, James shook his head as if to dismiss the reality of Nate not being there. Walking over to one of the metal file cabinets labeled dead files, he opened a drawer.

"Is there anything I can do to help you find what you're looking for?" Ray moved deeper into the room and leaned against the edge of a large metal desk.

"I just need some papers out of here," James answered flipping through the files looking for the one that he was seeking.

Finding it, he lifted the file folder from its place and was about to close the drawer when a sealed manila envelope behind the folder caught his attention. There was a large yellow post-it attached which read: *Take to California*. Written under those words was the date that Nate had flown into LAX. Looking puzzled, James pulled the envelope from the cabinet drawer.

"I wonder how that got back in there," he said absently.

"What?" Ray asked absent-mindedly as he glanced at his watch, anxious to leave so that they could meet Bev and Dana at the airport.

"I think that Nate meant to take this with him." James held the envelope up for Ray to see, and took the post-it off of the name that it was obscuring.

Ray became restless. "Hey man, we have to get going. It's getting late." He looked up to see James staring at him.

"What?"

James thrust the envelope toward Ray. He pointed to the two words printed neatly across it.

Ray read them and froze. The name written on the folder was his.

****

The house in which Gillian and Nia were held was located in the middle of a foreclosed farm. Sin hadn't appreciated how isolated the area was until he actually drove here.

Fields that should have been lush with crops were brown and barren, providing an unhampered view of the surrounding landscape. It was easy to spot anyone approaching the house from all directions. It was a perfect setting in which to keep two kidnapped children.

Sin walked around the boarded up house, fighting the urge to burn it to the ground. Starr had planned on coming here to see the place before his partner's untimely death, and Sin was to come with him. Since that plan was curtailed, he decided to come alone.

As luck would have it, an emergency at Sin's office forced him to leave Nedra and their children in Stillwaters sooner than expected. He flew back to the Peninsula, and while there, he was determined to stay in his own home.

Despite the weeks that had passed since the abduction, there was still a substantial media presence at the cul-de-sac entrance. Sin donned a Webb Starr uniform under the guise of being one of their employees in order to get back and forth to his house undisturbed.

Earlier today, after attending a meeting that lasted way too long, he shed his business attire, slipped into a pair of jeans and drove beyond the nearby city of Salinas to the infamous hostage house.

Sin wasn't satisfied by the still photos the authorities showed his family of this place. His curiosity wasn't satisfied. He wanted to see the house for himself.

Time had not diminished the rage he felt about the abduction. It consumed him. Nedra was satisfied that they had their daughter back and she wanted him to let the anger go. Sin knew that was impossible for him to do, not until justice was served.

Under the guise of being an investigator from Webb Starr, Sin followed up on calling the doctor whose name was on the prescription bottle in Vega's medicine cabinet. That turned out to be a dead end. The doctor worked in a clinic, and all Sin got out of him was that Vega wasn't a regular patient. The doctor didn't know if anyone ever accompanied him to his medical visits, and he didn't know anything else about him except that the prescription written for Vega was for allergies.

Since that was a bust, Sin was here today hoping that he could find something—anything—that would help with the case, although he doubted it. The house and the area surrounding it had been thoroughly examined. He was sure that not much had been missed. Still it didn't hurt to try.

The yellow tape put around the crime scene weeks ago was still there, weathered worn and flapping in the occasional breeze. The front door was boarded and a pad lock was attached. He assumed the same was true for the back door.

Following the dirt path around the perimeter of the house, Sin could see that it had been well traveled. Not only had the authorities walked this path, but so had the media, the paparazzi and a curious public. He was surprised there was no one else out here today.

When he reached the back he found that although the door was boarded, it wasn't padlocked. Sin shook his head. What was it with people leaving these backdoors so vulnerable? He studied the lock for a few seconds. It was a simple, singular cylinder. No problem.

Returning to his car, he looked through the tools in his trunk, found the perfect one and a flashlight and then returned to the back door. It took a few minutes for him to pick the lock. In his youth he could have been inside in less than sixty seconds. He was rusty.

Using the flashlight, he walked through the darkened house. As he wandered the place, light streamed through slits and knotholes in the plywood boards on the windows aiding his progress.

Stopping at the closet size room in which Gillian and Nia had been imprisoned only added fuel to the fire. He took photos of the room and of the bathroom from which they escaped. It made him more determined than ever to see that everyone involved in the kidnapping was caught.

****

James glanced across the aisle at Ray who was looking out of the airplane window. He appeared to be staring into space. Bev Cameron Walker was asleep on her husband's shoulder. She became aware of her husband's change in demeanor the moment Ray and James met her at the airport. She asked Ray what was wrong.

James knew that Ray was lying when he told her nothing. Whatever was bothering him had to do with the envelope that Ray asked him to put in his briefcase. It was obvious that he didn't want Bev to see the envelope.

James came to the conclusion that what was being transported inside his briefcase was information gathered from an investigation that Nate did for Ray. It must have been prior to the Webb Starr merger, because the file cabinet in which it was stashed contained Nate's old cases. James wasn't privy to the file cabinet's contents, but finding the envelope rattled Ray, and he had been subdued since its discovery.

James's eyes slid from Ray to Bev. This was the first time that he had met his friend's wife in person. Like Dana, her sister was very attractive. She was tall, sleek and as sophisticated as hell. She dressed expensively and every hair on her head was in place.

He knew that Bev was older than Ray, but James would have been hard-pressed to prove it. The women in Dana's family must have a fountain of youth stashed away, as well as magic wands, because they certainly knew how to cast a spell on a man. He had to admit that Dana had him practically wrapped up and tied with a bow.

There was no doubt that Ray was head over heels in love with his wife. That's why James suspected that whatever was in that envelope had something to do with her. Did Ray have her investigated? Someone in her family investigated? If so, who?

He was curious about what was in that envelope. Of course if he really wanted to know, he could easily find out. Technically, the envelope in his possession did belong to the agency and he could keep it. But, whatever was inside was important to Ray, and their friendship was more valuable than James' curiosity. Besides, although he hoped things would turn out well for Ray, he didn't have time to concern himself with whatever Ray was dealing with. He had to get back to investigating the kidnapping.

James looked up to find Dana watching him. He lifted a curious brow. She flashed a soft smile.

"What are you thinking about? Your expression is so solemn that I couldn't help but wonder."

He squeezed her hand. "I was thinking about how much I've got to do."

"You do have a lot on you."

Dana was quite aware of his burdens. Since he received the call about Nate, she had stayed by his side. She helped plan his partner's memorial service, and accompanied him to a meeting with his employees in which he assured them that despite Nate's death, the agency would continue. Dana was also there when he made arrangements to settle Nate's estate, and she helped clean out his apartment. James couldn't believe how generous and supportive she was being.

"Thank you." He placed a kiss on her forehead.

"What for?"

"For being the wonderful woman that you are.." His heart was full, and not only with feelings of gratitude. His feelings for Dana were beginning to become so much more.

"I appreciate that." She really did and she appreciated him even more.

During their time together, she got to see sides of James that endeared him to her in ways that he would never know. His strengths and his vulnerabilities had been revealed during this unexpected crisis, and she came to respect both. James was a man of action.

"What are you planning to do now?"

Dana didn't have to be specific. James knew what she meant. In the blink of an eye, his life became complicated, but he faced the challenges as they came. Before leaving New York City, he promoted one of his senior staff to manage the East Coast division of Webb Starr. Meanwhile, he still had plans to open the branch office in northern California.

"I've decided to bring one of my men to the Bay Area to help set up the operation there. I've got too many other things on my plate to pursue that, including working on the case for your family."

"Oh! What a privilege! We're being served by a CEO now." Dana elbowed him teasingly; glad to be able to provide some levity to their conversation. The last few days had been filled with so much sadness.

"I guess so," James struck a serious tone. Not only did he acquire a new title, but overnight he became a wealthy man.

Before Nate's death James made a comfortable living as a partner in their thriving business. But he was now its sole owner. Nate had no living relatives and left everything to him, including a substantial life insurance policy. James was shocked at how much. There had been a lot of surprises this past week, but Dana's steadfast support was what he valued most.

"I know I've said it before, but I can't thank you enough for being here with me." He paused to gain a hold on his errant emotions. "Other than Nate, nobody outside of my family has ever been there for me like this." He spoke across the aisle to Ray. "I want to thank you for your support too."

Hearing himself being addressed, Ray turned from the window and gave him a vacant smile. Dana squeezed James' hand, speaking for them both.

"We're glad that we were able to be here."

"I plan on returning the favor." James said with resolve. "I swear to you, if it's the last thing I do in life, I will help find everyone who was responsible for kidnapping those girls."

CHAPTER 20

It was late in the evening when the limo delivered James to the house in Tiburon. The rental contract with Ray had been signed and the house was officially his. The others passengers were dropped off at the houseboat. James promised to call Dana later.

Although he tried to express it, he doubted if Dana really understood how much her kindness and consideration during this past week meant to him. She didn't give herself credit for how thoughtful she could be. She didn't give herself credit for a lot of things, but he gave Dana high praise for how she made him feel.

James was finishing his dinner when the doorbell rang. It was Ray. James wasn't surprised. As soon as Ray walked through the front door, James handed him the envelope

Ray took a seat in the living room where James found him sitting on the sofa fingering the unopened envelope. James took a seat across from him.

Ray was in emotional turmoil. Years had passed since he hired Nathan Webb to investigate Bev's late husband, Colton Cameron. That resulted in the shocking discovery that the man faked his own death. Bev wasn't aware of that result, but when she accidently discovered that the investigation was being conducted, the revelation caused difficulties in their relationship.

Ray thought that he remedied the mistake of having initiated that search when he burned the copy of the report he was given. He vowed that he would take the secret of what was uncovered to his grave. He had no idea that Nate kept a copy of the results of that investigation.

Ray's reaction to the copy being on file was virulent. This left James wondering what was in the envelope that had Ray so upset.

"The firm routinely keeps file copies," James informed him calmly.

"Nate told me that he gave me the only copy. It looks like that wasn't true," Ray spat. He wondered why Nate would keep a copy, but since the man was dead, he would never know.

"Since the envelope is sealed and was in that particular file cabinet, I'm sure that nobody but Nate read the contents," James reassured him.

With those words Ray felt a little better. James seemed unaware of the envelope's existence until its discovery. Yet in a moment of paranoia, Ray wondered if finding the envelope really was a coincidence. It was a thought that he quickly dismissed.

At this point all Ray could do was pray there were no other copies and that no one else on earth knew what he knew about Colton Cameron. The reality of that man's continued existence would impact far too many lives, including his own. From what Ray learned, Colton Cameron was not a man to be taken lightly.

James watched the conflict of emotions playing across his friend's face. He had no clue what was in that envelope, but its contents was causing him a lot of distress. After what Ray did for him in New York, James was ready to help him if he could.

"Are you in trouble? Is there anything I can do?"

Ray flashed a grateful smile. "No, I'm okay. I was just thinking about coincidences. "

"In some instances, they can be the best thing that can happen to you." James offered. It had been a startling coincidence—if not a miracle—that brought Dana into his life.

"Or it can be the worst thing possible." Ray thought about the twist of fate that caused him to stumble on the secret about Colton Cameron.

"Whatever the case," James reflected, "Coincidences do happen, and for reasons that I'm sure we human beings will never understand."

****

Hardman made certain the gun was firmly in place in his pocket as he stood on the side of the road in the desolate countryside. His rental car had a flat tire and he was as mad as hell. Being the product of big cities, he knew nothing about barren places like this with its miles and miles of farmland interrupted by occasional houses, none of which he could see at the moment. Nightfall was rapidly approaching. He hoped that some wild animal didn't attack him before he fixed the damn tire. It seemed as though the impromptu decision he made earlier today might not have been a good one.

Using the information he procured from Andy Vega, he drove up the coast to the Monterey Peninsula to the city of Salinas. This was where the ringleader of the three kidnappers was supposed to be residing. Hardman had been watching the man's house for nearly a week. So far, the guy hadn't made an appearance, but Hardman remained hopeful.

It was Hardman's curiosity that led him to this two lane road on which he was stranded. For some reason he was compelled to see for himself where the girls had been held. He decided that it would be best to take this side trip late in the day to avoid coming in contact with anyone. That proved to be prophetic. He hadn't seen another car or human being since his tire went flat.

Where was help when you needed it? He had never changed a tire in his life.

Sin pressed his foot down on the accelerator and felt the power of his luxury vehicle gliding along the deserted road. He didn't want to be caught in this desolate area at night. He liked quiet and solitude, but this was a bit too much. He couldn't wait to get home.

Turning up his music, he slid the car into cruise and settled back to enjoy the ride. He should be in Carmel in about an hour. Later, he would call Nedra and the kids. Dana, Ray and Starr were back in the Bay Area by now. He would give them calls as well.

Deep in thought about his visit to the kidnap house, he passed the car on the opposite side of the road without a glance. It wasn't until he looked into the rear view mirror and saw the lone figure of a man kneeling beside the car that he realized the vehicle wasn't abandoned. Night was rapidly approaching. He felt sorry for anybody stuck out here in no man's land, but he didn't have time to be a Good Samaritan. He wanted to get home.

Hardman was beside himself. Damn! The only car on the road and he let it pass by. He was so preoccupied with trying to read the manual and figure out how to get the tire off of the rim that he hadn't heard it coming. By the time he became aware of the vehicle's presence it had sped pass. He watched the tail lights disappear down the road.

There was no time to lament. He had to get the tire changed before it got dark.

Hardman was about to return to his place beside the flat tire when he looked up to see a car coming. It was on the same side of the road this time and moving slowly. Hope sprang anew, mingled with a tinge of anxiety.

Stepping onto the road, he waved his arms to get the driver's attention. If the car stopped, he hoped, for the sake of whoever was driving, that any intentions were good ones. The car pulled up behind his and stopped.

Sin wanted to kick himself a thousand times as he turned off the engine. Until now he didn't know to what extent Nedra had brainwashed him with all of her do-good stuff. He was in the middle of nowhere, stopping to help what could well be a mass murderer, and nobody even knew where he was.

Oh, what the hell! It could be him stuck out here—but, just in case. Before getting out of the car, he removed the gun from its ankle holster and placed it in his jacket pocket.

The man standing at the back of the disabled vehicle was putting on his jacket as Sin approached. The stranger was African-American, and looked quite distinguished. Sin guessed his age to be in the late fifties or early sixties. He was medium height with a slim build. The clothes he wore were casual, but expensive. It was obvious that he didn't belong in these parts. Sin wondered what the guy was doing out here, plus he didn't look too well. He looked as though he was seeing a ghost.

Stunned, Hardman watched the stranger walking toward him. He knew that face! He knew the dark eyes, the sharp cheek bones, the broad nose, the cleft chin. As a boy he caressed that face and smothered it with kisses. It was the face of the man who he loved fiercely, the man who helped his mother raise him. It was his grandfather's face, except his grandfather was dead!

Sin slowed his steps, not wanting to spook the man any further. Was he sick? Was he frightened? What was wrong?

"Hello. I passed you out here and thought that you might need help." Sin held his hand out to the stranger in greeting. "My name is Sinclair Reasoner."

Hardman swayed. His heart began to race. He felt dizzy. He could hardly breathe. He had to get a hold of himself. He couldn't pass out. He needed to exert some self-control. But how could he? Never! *Never* in his wildest dreams would he have expected to have something like this happen!

Sin took a quick step forward. Was the man having a heart attack? "Are you all right? You look ill."

Steadying himself, Hardman cleared his throat, forcing himself to focus. It wasn't easy.

"No, no I'm okay." He took a shaky breath. "It's just that I'm stuck out here in no man's land with a flat tire. Night is coming fast and my phone battery is low, so I couldn't call for help." Attempting to regain his equilibrium, he exhaled. "I'm Tom Hardman. I'm glad that you stopped." He shook Sin's hand. "Thank you."

"No problem," Sin transferred his attention to the flat tire on the back passenger side of the car.

A jack and the donut spare lay on the ground next to an open manual. Sin suspected that this man had no clue what he was doing. His speech and manner were cultured. More than likely he was a business executive, and not an average working stiff.

"Looks like you do need help." Sin took his tailor made jacket off.

"I'm not exactly handy when it comes to things like this," Hardman admitted.

Sin chuckled. "Well, I've changed a tire or two in my time." Folding his jacket neatly, he placed it inside Hardman's open car trunk. "There's still enough light for me to get this done. If you'll just hand me the tools, we can get started. "

"Sure," Hardman followed him around the car. He was as nervous as a preacher in a whore house. The cool façade that he once mastered had completely vanished.

Sin bent to look at the tire. So far all Mr. Hardman managed to do was raise the car with the jack. Using the tire iron Sin removed the hub cap.

"Did you set the emergency brake?" Sin asked before going any farther.

Looking guilty, Hardman hurried around to the driver's side of the car and set the brake. Returning to take his place beside Sin, he watched with admiration as he removed the lugs.

Sinclair worked with swift precision. Hardman couldn't take his eyes off of him. There were a million questions that he wanted to ask him, so many that he wouldn't know where to start.

He did notice that when he got out of the car, Sinclair approached him with measured caution. That meant that he wasn't the type of man to be caught off guard. Naiveté wasn't a part of the man's character. He assessed a situation before stepping into it. Hardman liked that, and he sensed that even while Sinclair was on the ground, with his back turned to a stranger, he wasn't as vulnerable as he might appear.

As he placed the spare on the rim, Sin could feel himself being scrutinized, but he didn't sense that he was in danger. Actually, Hardman appeared to be enthralled by what he was doing. He was watching him in awe.

Sin didn't see the big deal. The guy probably never saw a tire being changed before. He didn't look like the type to have engaged in manual labor. He was curious about Mr. Hardman.

"I hope that you don't mind my asking, but what are you doing out here in this deserted place?"

Hardman hesitated. He knew that he couldn't tell him the truth, but Sinclair seemed astute and might pick up on a lie. He ventured a half truth.

"I got lost." That part was true. He had gotten lost several times trying to find the road to that damn kidnap house. "My GPS must not be working.

Sin nodded, realizing that was the extent of the information that was going to be provided. "I see."

The conversation was interrupted by the ringing of a telephone. Sin's head whipped around to his car.

"That's my cell. I left it on the front seat." Rising, he started toward his car. "Will you tighten the rest of those lug nuts? I'll come back and check them before we put the hub cap back on." Indicating to Hardman the tool to be used, Sin went to answer the call.

Hardman watched his panther like retreat. *He even walks like my grandfather.* His mouth curved into a pensive smile.

Sin reached into the car window and retrieved his phone. Darnell was on the other end. "Hey, Sis," Sin greeted her call with a grin. He was glad to hear from her. Their progression from cousins by marriage to siblings by blood had turned into a relationship they both cherished.

"Hi, big brother. I spoke to Mama and Ray. They're back in the Bay Area. I think my call interrupted some serious business, if you know what I mean."

"Oh, you're so bad."

"She shouldn't have answered the telephone. I wouldn't have. Would you?"

They shared a laugh. His sister was a crazy woman, but he loved her to death.

"Anyhow, Mama mumbled something about Dana being on the houseboat with them, and she said that James Starr is living in Tiburon. What's he doing in Tiburon? Isn't he supposed to be in L.A. or on the Peninsula looking for the kidnappers?"

"It's my understanding that Starr is in Tiburon because he's moving into Ray's old house—you know the one that your husband used to live in," he reminded her jokingly. Before Thad and Darnell were married and they moved to Carmel, she used to spend a lot of time at that house. "So don't worry, Starr was hired to help find the scum and I have no doubt that he will."

From the discomfort of the hard ground where he was suppose to be tightening the lugs, Hardman watched surreptitiously as Sin leaned against the front of his car and talked on the cell phone. He noted the long, lean lines of his tall, well toned body and the confidence of his stance. It was a marvel, as if his grandfather had come to life. He looked and moved just like him.

In the eerie silence of the countryside, Hardman could hear snatches of Sinclair's side of the conversation, and discerned that he was talking to Darnell. He also managed to hear enough to figure out that someone named Starr had been hired to catch "the scum", who kidnapped the girls. Darnell had warned them publicly that she would have someone on their case until they were caught. She was proving as good as her word. Hot damn! That was his girl!

Finished with the lugs, Hardman tossed the flat tire into the trunk. He looked around in time to see Sinclair approaching.

"You're all finished?" He walked around to the side of the car, hunkered down and checked the lugs. "They look good." Replacing the hubcap, he took the car off the jack and stood to face Hardman. "All set." He handed Hardman the jack and tire iron, which he placed in the trunk before closing it.

Turning to Sin, Hardman held his dirty hand out to shake Sinclair's filthy one. "I can't thank you enough. I'd like to offer you some mon…"

"Don't insult me." Sin pumped the man's hand heartily. "I'm sure you would have done the same for me."

"Then may I buy you a drink? Dinner maybe?" He didn't want to let him go.

"No, I'm good."

Sin's phone rang again. He looked at caller ID.

"It's my wife," he told Hardman apologetically.

"Okay." Hardman started backing away. "I'd better get out of here." He looked at the darkened sky. "It's getting late, so thank you again."

"No sweat," Sin started backing toward his own car. With one last wave, he turned away.

Hardman got into his car and made a u-turn. Sin was standing by his car talking on his phone. Hardman didn't speed away until he saw Sin's car lights come on, and through his rear view mirror observe the pattern of his car lights making a similar u- turn and head his way.

Sinclair's car followed Hardman's until they both reached the Salinas city limits. It wasn't until the two men approached the highway entrance that they turned and went in two different directions.

CHAPTER 21

When James opened the front door the next morning Dana was standing there posing. Wearing a bright orange trench coat and carrying a matching umbrella, her outfit, along with her dazzling smile, brighten a grey and rainy day. The previous evening, when they spoke on the telephone they made arrangement to eat breakfast together at his house.

"Good morning." She gave him a peck on the lips.

"Good morning to you." James closed the door behind her and helped her out of her coat. He hung it in the closet, while she placed the wet umbrella in the tiled foyer. Encircling her waist, he held her loosely in his embrace. "Now you can give me a real good morning kiss."

"If you insist."

She softly brushed her lips across his, enticing them to part. Once inside, the tip of her tongue explored the cozy corners that had become all too familiar, she lovingly sparred with his tongue in a battle for control. The kiss deepened. It lingered, promising the possibility of a future that could include each other.

"Wow! That's what I call a kiss."

"I can feel your appreciation." Dana's hand grazed his groin.

"That's right, and if you kiss me like this again, we won't be getting to breakfast until lunch time."

She flashed a wicked grin. "Is that a promise?"

Woman, you better believe it is." He guided her toward the kitchen. "I better get you in here while I can still walk."

"He enjoyed their sexual repartee, and the idea of making love to her right there in the foyer was an inviting one, but he didn't want Dana to think that his only interest in her was sexual. She meant more to him than that.

Dana was escorted into the brightly colored kitchen where she emitted a squeal of delight. James had set the table with a linen table cloth, matching napkins and a single lit candle. Two crystal goblets held glasses of orange juice and placed on two decorative plates were two wrapped breakfast sandwiches from a fast food restaurant.

"I cooked for hours," James quipped.

They delved into their sandwiches, enjoying the pleasure of being together. This giant of a man was nothing like the ones that Dana previously dated. He came from the streets and fought his way to his present position. James lived life on his own terms. Yet, he was open and easy going, a direct contradiction to his looming presence. She had to admit that she could see herself falling hard for this man.

"What are you thinking?" he asked.

"I was thinking about how I could learn to like having breakfast with you like this in the mornings."

James liked her answer, but he didn't respond to what she said right away. Finishing his sandwich, he washed it down with the rest of his juice, wiped his mouth and sat back to focus on Dana.

"We seem to have a good thing going, and I like it. I don't want to lose it. When we were on the plane flying back here, I got to thinking about Nate and how I watched him make work his priority for years. Women came in and out of his life, but I don't ever remember him talking about anybody seriously. If a woman came into his life who took up too much of his time, she was dumped. I think that he was scared of commitment, and of anything he couldn't control."

"Did he have a lot of control over you?" Dana couldn't conceive of anyone being able to hold any power over this bear of a man.

"In a way he did. I worshipped him and he knew it. I rarely challenged him. I followed every step he suggested I take, and ended up the better for it, so I can't complain."

"I hear a *but*."

"But, I don't want to end up like he did at the end— alone. I've known the joy of having a family and the pain of losing one, but even knowing how much that pain can hurt, I'm still willing to give that chance at joy one more try with you."

Dana was both touched and surprised by his admission. James wasn't the type of man to put his heart on the line like this. It wouldn't be fair to him if she was less candid.

"I've told you that I'm scared, James. We both agreed that we need time to let this relationship develop."

"We're still on the same page." James rested his muscled arms on the table and leaned toward Dana. "I just wanted to let you know that I'm willing to do whatever it takes so that our relationship can develop. I don't want to make a mistake with us."

"I don't either. I want a mutual commitment, like Ray and my sister have."

"I wouldn't want anything less."

James was a witness to the couple's devotion to each other when they were together in New York. He saw it yesterday when Ray agonized over the contents of the envelope that was discovered in Nate's office.

It wasn't difficult for James to guess that whatever was in that package could in some way involve Ray's wife. Without sharing the details of what was inside, Ray had asked James a question that made him ponder the complexities of a relationship.

"What would you do if you had to make a choice between truth and love?"

"That's a hard one, so let me think about it," James told him. They shared a glass of wine and some chit chat before James was ready to address the question.

"If the truth cost me the love, then I'd chose love," he finally answered.

Ray gave James a noncommittal smile, but didn't respond. James excused himself to make a few phone calls, and when he returned to the living room Ray asked if he could use his paper shredder.

James watched as Ray meticulously removed the pages from the manila envelope. Never glancing at one single sheet of paper, he destroyed each page, one by one. After the last page was shred, the remnants were placed in a plastic trash bag and put out with the garbage for pickup.

Before he left for the evening, Ray told James, "I'm going to let truth take care of itself."

"You're not listening to me."

James started. Dana was right. His mind was somewhere else.

"I'm sorry. I was thinking about a question that someone asked me recently and I'd like to hear your opinion."

Finishing the last of her sandwich, Dana tossed her napkin aside. "Okay, what is it?"

"What would you do if you had to make a choice between truth and love?"

Dana's eyes searched his face. Was he trying to tell her something? Had he been dishonest with her?

She caught herself. There it was. She was doing it again. Questioning. Suspecting. Doubting. She did the same things in her past relationships, the unsuccessful ones. If she wanted this one to be different, she had to approach it differently. James merely asked a question, and from the expectant look on his face, it was clear that her answer was important to him because he valued her opinion. She mulled the question over thoughtfully.

"That's a tricky one. I think that it would depend on the situation. Not telling the truth can mean having a lack of integrity, and that's no good. Yet, if that truth would hurt someone or ruin a relationship, then I would probably choose love."

"And you would let truth take care of itself?"

"Yes," Dana echoed. "I'd let truth take care of itself."

****

Hardman had barely slept. Even the arrival of a new day, couldn't quell the feeling of excitement about his encounter with Sinclair Reasoner. He didn't believe in a Higher Power, so he doubted that what happened yesterday was the result of divine intervention. As for karma, if there was such a thing, he had no idea why it would have worked so perfectly for him. He could only conclude that it was the incredible luck that had followed him throughout his life that brought him the good fortune that he knew he didn't deserve.

Good deeds were never a part of that life. The vast wealth he accumulated, illegally, helped him wield the power he gained with ruthless intent. He destroyed anyone who got in his way. He used his fortune to bribe, extort, coerce and even worse. Most important, his wealth was used, more than once, to save his own life.

Acquiring aliases was his specialty. Over the years he had gone by so many names that he wasn't sure who he really was anymore.

Only once, as an adult, did he live like a normal human being. That was when he was with Bev. He could truly say that when he was married to her, that was the happiest time in his adult life, but their time together was brief.

Because of his illicit activities, his life was threatened and he was forced to abandon his young wife to save her life and that of their unborn child. It was the most difficult decision that he ever had to make.

After surgically altering his appearance, he became someone else—the first time. With a brand new face and a brand new life, he rose to the height of power in the underworld, where he had made enemies. Lady luck smiled on him again when a trusted employee helped Hardman escape his fate the second time. It was that turn of events that took him to the island paradise where he lived a close to perfect life.

Now, here he was, a man who didn't exist. The life that he led would not have made his beloved grandfather proud. Yet he felt a sense of redemption. Despite his unsavory past, there were two human beings in this world who made up for his many improprieties. They were both decent people who were making their marks in the world. He couldn't be more pleased or proud.

It was even more satisfying because he was certain that his initial suspicion about Sinclair being a fraud proved to be unfounded. After seeing him, Hardman still had no idea who his mother might be, but there was absolutely no doubt in his mind who fathered Sinclair Reasoner.

CHAPTER 22

"I took pictures of the place," Sin informed Nedra as he sat in his office recounting his trip to the kidnapper's hideout. "Don't ask me why..."

"I know why," Nedra said wisely. "You need them to keep fueling your anger."

"No," he tried to deny. "Starr might need them to..."

"Starr? James Starr? What has he got to do with this?"

"Nedra..."

"If he needed pictures why didn't he go take them? He doesn't need you to play amateur detective."

"Listen, Nedra..."

"You listen! You need to let this go, Sinclair. Your only concern should be helping us get home so that this family can be together again, not chasing criminals trying to get revenge. I *know* you, and I know that's what you're doing!"

Sin became defensive. "You don't understand..."

"Yes, I do! I understand that you need to use common sense and not street sense to get us home." Nedra was perturbed. "Just be glad that you've got a daughter who was bright enough to outsmart full grown adults and get away! Be grateful for that and leave finding those idiots to the authorities, and to James Starr."

Sin didn't answer. Nedra knew that meant he would continue with his stubborn pursuit. Since she was getting nowhere, she abruptly changed the subject.

"How are things between Dana and James? Bev told me that they looked like they were getting hot and heavy in New York."

Sin navigated those waters carefully. "I don't know."

His answer was as close as he could get to being honest. He hadn't talked to Dana or James since they got back, and he was grateful when Nedra dropped the subject. After speaking to his children, he disconnected and got back to work.

Since his return to the Peninsula, things hadn't slowed down at his import company. One emergency after another materialized, each requiring his attention and presence at the office and preventing him from getting back to his family.

He was reviewing some forms when his administrative assistant buzzed him.

"There's a Mr. Hardman here to see you."

The name drew a blank. "Does he have an appointment?"

"He says that he met you last night and that he has something for you that you might have missed."

That refreshed Sin's memory. "Send him in."

He stood as the man from the desolate road entered his office. Like Sin, he was no longer dressed casually. The suit he wore was finely tailored, the shirt custom-made, and the tie was of fine silk. Today, he looked more like the wealthy CEO Sin envisioned him to be, and he was carrying a neatly wrapped package.

"Mr. Hardman, how good to see you again." They shook hands. Sin noticed that the man's hand was clammy and there was a slight tremor. Once again, Sin wondered about his health. "Please, have a seat, and if you'll excuse me a moment, I have to take some papers across the hall. I'll be right back."

"No problem." Hardman settled in one of the chairs across from Sinclair's desk.

When Sinclair left the room Hardman exhaled. It was unsettling being in the room with an exact replica of his late grandfather. It was as though he had come back to life.

He never expected to see Sinclair Reasoner again. After he took care of the man in Salinas, his plan was to leave northern California, and return to L.A. where he would take a flight out of the country and return to his island paradise a satisfied man.

His trip to the States had garnered more than he could have ever imagined. He never expected more. Yet when he opened the trunk of his rental car this morning and discovered Sinclair's jacket inside, he was delighted. Fate had provided him with an excuse to see his son again.

As he sat in Sinclair's office, Hardman caught his breath at the sight of a cornucopia of family photographs sitting on a side table. Rising, he walked over to them and stared.

There was a silver framed photo of Sinclair with a brown skinned beauty with amazing light brown eyes. From the way the two looked at each other it wasn't difficult to speculate that the woman was his wife. Another picture showed Sinclair and his wife posed with three beautiful children, two boys and a girl. He didn't know the boys' names, but he knew that the young girl with the impish grin had to be the infamous Gillian. There were individual photos of each of the children, and then the series of photos changed.

Hardman had to grip the table to remain steady as he gazed at a photograph of Bev. He began to tremble as he looked into the eyes of the woman who still remained the love of his life—Bev

Even today her name sent tremors of desire through his system. He remembered her telling him that no one ever called her Beverly, and he fell for her the moment that they met. Never had he loved one human being so completely, and she was as lovely in this photo as she was when they were both young, and their worlds revolved around each other.

He studied her face like an artist would a rare painting. He had read that she remarried. He couldn't recall the man's name, but he was glad that she had gone on with her life. Happiness and joy were the only things that he ever wanted for her. She was the only woman in his life who had given him both.

In the photograph, Bev was posed with Darnell and a little girl—Nia. The little girl resembled her mother, but peered at him with eyes that strangely enough were carbon copies of Sinclair's wife. The dimpled cheek smile was that of her father's. Nia Campbell Stewart was gorgeous, a perfect combination of her famous parents.

Hardman swallowed the lump in his throat. He was about to lose it. That was a certainty when he looked at the last of the photographs. It was a candid snapshot of Darnell and Sinclair together. They were walking along the beach, looking at each other, laughing at some shared experience. Perhaps it was the delight of having found each other—at least that was what Hardman wanted to imagine.

With shaky hands, he withdrew a tiny video camera from his pocket. Grateful for modern technology, he recorded the row of photographs and had just put the camera away, when Sinclair walked back into the office.

"Sorry about that."

"I've got to go to the restroom." Hardman exited the office hurriedly.

"Third door on the left," Sin called after him.

Standing in the bathroom, Hardman waited until the quivers in his body subsided. Wetting a paper towel, he wiped his tear-stained face. Once he gathered himself, he patted his jacket pocket, reassuring himself that the treasured video camera was secure, and then he returned to Sinclair's office.

While Hardman was gone, Sin retrieved the package that was left on his desk. His jacket was folded neatly. The gun was still in the pocket. When Hardman returned, the two men gave each other a knowing look.

"I want to thank you for returning my property, Mr. Hardman I didn't miss it until I was almost home, and by that time it was too late. I didn't know how to get in touch with you, so I figured that I would never see it again."

"It's a nice jacket, and since I wanted to make sure that you got everything you owned, I thought it best to bring it directly to you."

Sin nodded, understanding his meaning. "I appreciate that, but I'm curious. How did you find me?"

"You told me your name and I looked you up on the internet," he told him truthfully. That's where I found the name and address of your business. There's not much that you can't find on the internet."

"That's true."

Sin flashed a smile so much like the one Hardman's grandfathers used to grace him with that Hardman had to divert his attention. He nodded toward the photos that he examined earlier.

"I was looking at the pictures over there. I assume that's your family?"

Warning bells went off in Sin's head. If this man was astute enough to look him up, then he probably knew about the kidnapping and that he was the father and uncle of the victims. But, he didn't take Mr. Hardman to be a reporter. Not many of them wore suits worth thousands of dollars, but it was best to be cautious.

"Yes, that's my wife and my kids."

"And the other ladies?"

"Relatives."

Hardman liked Sinclair's discretion. Under the right circumstance, what a team the two of them could have made. He tested him further.

"The woman in that picture there looks like the singer, Darnell Cameron." He indicated the photo of Darnell with her mother and daughter.

"Yes, she does." Sin sensed that Hardman was aware that it was Darnell.

Hardman knew that he knew that the photo was of Darnell, and was testing him. This man was savvy. Like himself, he played his cards close to his chest.

Feeling his emotions threatening to get the best of him again, reluctantly Hardman rose to leave. "I'd better go, Mr. Reasoner."

"Call me Sinclair."

"All right, Sinclair. But, I hope that you don't mind if I ask you a question."

Sin was guarded. "Go ahead."

"Why would you need to carry a gun?"

Sin didn't flinch. "Why would *you* need to carry one?"

Hardman was caught off guard, and that didn't happen often. When they met he was carrying a weapon, in a holster at the small of his back. Only the most perceptive observer would have known it was there.

"You put your jacket on when I approached."

Sin gave no further explanation. He didn't need to. Hardman understood what was being said.

His son had been aware that the stranger on the road was concealing a weapon. Yet he helped him despite it. That took courage and confidence. Hell no! That took guts! Man, he really liked this guy. Not only that, but he respected him. His coming to see him only confirmed the decision that he had been mulling over this morning about what to do about the last kidnapper.

He held his hand out for a parting shake. "Sinclair, I can't tell you how very good it was to meet you."

Sin noted the admiration in his voice. "Thank you, Mr. Hardman. I'm glad that I could help, and I really appreciate your returning my things."

Hardman gave a final nod, and he left. Sin continued going through some paperwork with nothing more on his mind than getting his family home.

****

It was raining in the San Francisco Bay area when Hardman arrived. All the way from the Peninsula he thought of nothing but the time that he spent with Sinclair. He reviewed every detail, every word, and every gesture. He played scenarios in his head about what would have happened if he told him who he was. Would he believe him? Colton Cameron was supposed to be dead. Would he hate him? Like him? He might have shot him. Hardman had no doubt that the man could handle a gun.

Everything he learned about Sinclair Reasoner during their two brief meetings he liked. He was cool, calm, and very smart. By displaying a picture of his sister without her husband, he could have her photo on display and still be discrete about her identity as he had been today. Hot damn! His son was a genius!

As he drove across the Golden Gate Bridge, Hardman realized that he hadn't felt this good in a long time. For once in his life he was about to do the right thing.

He didn't know who this guy Starr was that he heard Sinclair talking about, but from what Hardman discerned from the conversation this was the man who was hired to pursue the kidnapping case.

Since Sinclair had been coming from the direction of the house where Hardman was headed before the flat stopped him, he assumed that his son was doing some investigating of his own. If Sinclair and this Starr guy were working together—and he highly suspected that might be the case—it was his hope that what he was about to do should lead to some sort of resolution to the abduction, and soon.

After taking the Tiburon exit, Hardman counted on GPS and his memory to guide him to the street and the house in which the man named Starr now resided. If anybody had asked him how he knew the exact location, he never would have confessed, but the truth was that he spent time in this area when Thad Stewart owned the house.

At the time Hardman was on a deadly mission. When he found out about Darnell's relationship with Thad, Hardman didn't feel that the superstar actor was good enough for his daughter. He planned on solving the problem permanently.

He was glad that plan fell through. Thad turned out to be perfect for Darnell, and Hardman wasn't proud of how he could have altered their future. At least today he could take pride in what he was about to do. Finding the house, he parked in front of it and got out.

He took pains not to leave fingerprints on the envelope that he held in his hand. He was a dead man and planned on staying that way. With gloved hands, he placed the envelope in the mail box and returned to his car.

Making a u-turn, he drove out of the neighborhood undetected. From now on he was leaving the rest of what had to be done up to the man named Starr and to his son, Sinclair Reasoner.

CHAPTER 23

As she lay in the large bed that she shared with James last night, Dana didn't know if she would ever wipe the smile off of her face. Incredible was the only word that she could think of to describe their experience. Never had she been made loved to so sensually, so sensationally, so sexually and without penetration.

The day started with breakfast and good conversation. They were both enjoying themselves until she broke the news to James that she would be leaving for L.A. in a few days.

"Despite the pestering media, I have to return to my office. Plus, I have a brand new condo that I was trying to settle into before all of this craziness happened. To say nothing of the fact that I'm still trying to sell the one that you moved out of." She had a life to resume, but this time she hoped that it would include him.

Her announcement sparked a serious discussion between them about what it would take for them to build a long distance relationship. They discussed the pros and cons, and eventually they reached the conclusion that what was developing between them was well worth the effort of exploring the possibility that their relationship could grow.

Since Dana was leaving the day after tomorrow, they wanted to spend as much time together as they could. The rest of the day was spent shopping for knick knacks that would turn James' house into a home. On the spur of the moment, they boarded the ferry to San Francisco.

In the city they dined on Fisherman's Wharf and then rode the cable car downtown. Dana never would have guessed that the solemn giant that she had come to know not only was spontaneous, but he liked to shop as much as she did. She was in heaven.

They arrived back in Tiburon in the late evening, wet and chilled from the day's steady rain. James asked if she would spend the night with him, and she eagerly agreed. She was downstairs accepting the delivery of the Chinese carryout that they ordered for dinner when he called to her from upstairs. Answering his call, she found him in the master bathroom where he had drawn a hot bath for her.

"It'll take away the chill," he promised.

Scented candles lit the bathroom and the bedroom. Romantic music was playing to help set the mood.

James bathed her with a slow and gentle hand. He took particular care to stroke all of the places that might need special attention. After she was bathed, he dried her with a thick, fluffy towel and proceeded to give an erotic massage.

The jasmine scented oil that he used permeated the air, and when his large hands delicately mapped her body with exquisite skill, Dana thought that she would burst into flames. His talented fingers dabbled with the secret places within her heated cove, and brought her to completion over and over again.

Later, Dana fell asleep in an exhilarated stupor, wrapped in James' strong arms. It was the perfect end to a very perfect day.

The next morning as she waited for James to return to the bedroom with yesterday's reheated carryout, Dana thought of how he made the night before all about her pleasure. She would never forget how very special he made her feel. James Starr was turning out to be an unexpected gift in her life.

Wrapped in a terry cloth robe, he walked through the door carrying a tray with two plates and the cartons filled with food.

"Good morning sleepy head. Come join me on the balcony." He motioned toward the closed French doors. "Will you do the honors?"

"I most certainly will." Dana scrambled from the bed and padded across the room to open the door for him.

"You're asking for trouble." His glittering eyes swept her nude form.

"Let's hope." Dana gave him a look as old as Eve in the Garden of Eden.

James sniggered at her antics. "Please do me a favor and go put some clothes on before I have a heart attack."

Dana took her time sashaying to the bathroom. She showered quickly and then donned one of his t-shirts which was much too large.

Stepping out on the balcony where James was seated at the patio table, she was pleased to find that the rain of the previous day had been replaced by bright sunshine. The fog had lifted and the day was pleasantly mild.

James was engrossed in reading a piece of paper in his hand. He looked up when she entered and emitted a throaty laugh. "I like your outfit." He wiggled his eyebrows at the oversized ensemble.

"I'm glad you do." She gave him a quick kiss, sat down across from him and started filling her plate. "What's that?" She indicated the paper in his hand.

"A note I found in the mailbox." He tossed it on the table and began filling his plate from the cartons.

She glanced at the piece of paper. "You're getting mail already?"

"Well, my staff knows where I am, but this letter wasn't mailed to me. The envelope just has Mr. Starr written across it."

Dana speared a piece of sesame chicken and was about to eat when her eye caught the first few words on the page. Putting the fork aside, she picked the paper up and continued reading. Typed on the sheet beside a man's name were the words: THE THIRD KIDNAPPER.

"What does this mean? I know that what this says can't be true. This is too easy."

"Exactly!" James chewed and swallowed. "And if you'll notice not only is a man's name provided but an address as well. I say this is just a little too convenient."

"The address is in Salinas," Dana observed. "That's about fifty miles from the house where the girls were held!" She looked at James. "Did one of your men put this in your mailbox or what?"

"No, none of my men would ever pull a stunt like that, not if they wanted to stay employed."

Dana frowned. "If it wasn't one of them, then who else would put this in your mailbox? The only people who know that you're working on this case are your employees, a few people in the FBI, and my family members. I know none of them wrote it. As a matter of fact, who in the FBI would know where you're living? You didn't tell Agent Conway did you?"

James shook his head in the negative, but her question stoked his curiosity.

"Maybe Carla brought it by. She knows that I'm here. It might be one of those letters that she keeps getting from strangers. But, if she dropped it off why didn't she come in?"

Abandoning his meal, James went into the house with Dana on his heels. Retrieving his cell phone, he called Carla. Meanwhile, Dana's cell phone began ringing. Sin answered her greeting.

"How did it go in New York?"

"It was hard on James, but he made it through.

How are things with you and yours?"

"Everybody is anxious to get home. Nedra and I have decided to bring Gillian and Trevor back to Carmel. They've spent enough time away from their home. They need some semblance of normalcy."

"If you think that's best."

"It is. Have you spoken to Darnell?"

"No," Dana felt guilty. Darnell, Thad and Nia were in Michigan spending time with his parents. "I haven't spoken to her in a few days. I'll call her today."

"Well she's wondering when Starr is going to get back to investigating the case, and so am I."

By the time James disconnected from his call, Dana had filled Sin in on the mysterious note. He wanted to know the name and the address written in the note, but her glimpse was brief and she couldn't remember either.

"Wait a minute, Sin. James is through talking to Carla. He can tell you what you want to know. Maybe Carla knows something about the note."

Hearing her comment, James mouthed, "She doesn't."

"Tell him that," she mouthed back to James before relinquishing her cell phone to him and hurrying off to the bathroom.

"Hey man," James said solemnly. He really didn't want to have this conversation with Sin, but since Dana spilled the beans about the note he knew that Sinclair wasn't going to let it go. "I know that Dana told you about the little mystery that we have here, but since Carla doesn't know anything about it, I'm not taking it seriously."

Sin wasn't happy about that decision. "I would think that you would follow up on every lead!"

"Every *legitimate* lead, yes, but this might be some sort of hoax. It's too cut and dry. Besides, I've got too much on my plate right now to go on a wild goose chase."

"It hasn't been proven that the last note was a hoax."

"No, and it hasn't been proved that it wasn't."

"Andy Vega knew Jack Spencer," Sin reminded James. "There must be some connection."

"And the FBI will find it. They have more manpower. I'll pass this note on to them and they can check it out."

"If manpower is the problem, then give me the name and address. I can check it out for you." Sin understood the man's position as a professional, but for him this was personal.

James gave a frustrated sigh. "Sin, it's a hoax."

"You don't know that! Dana said that you both have questions about why the note was put in *your* mailbox. How in the hell would someone playing a hoax even know where you're staying, let alone that you're working on the case? Obviously, it isn't a coincidence that the note was put in your mailbox. Somebody has found out that you're working for us, and they're giving you a lead." Sin's voice had hardened. "And it's a lead that you're being well paid to follow."

Sin was no longer annoyed he was angry. He wanted that name and address.

James knew that he would have to handle this situation with finesse. Any semblance of a relationship that he and Sin had established was tenuous at best. He didn't want to fracture it completely.

"I'm also being paid to handle this case my way," he countered, "and right now this is the way I want to handle it."

Sin took a calming breath. "I don't understand the problem, Starr. You followed the lead when that other note came to you. Hell, we looked like a group of vigilantes swooping down on Vega's house. Now, all of a sudden, I've got to practically beg you to follow up on this?"

Dana stepped out of the bathroom. The strained look on James' face alerted her that his talk with Sin wasn't going well. She sat down beside him.

James tried to be conciliatory. "Man, you're a loose cannon and you need to take a step back..."

"I don't think that's for you to say," Sin snapped.

"Well, that's my opinion," James answered calmly. "So, with that I'll say good-bye. I'll talk to you later." He hung up.

"What's going on?" Dana queried.

"Sin wants the information in that note, and I won't give it to him because I know that he'll follow-up on it. I really don't need him in my way while I'm trying to do my job."

"Do you really think that he'll be in the way? You let all of us go with you when we went to Vega's house."

"You were there because you were my ticket into his house, but as you might recall I was reluctant to take you with me.. I really shouldn't have let any of you go. Anything could have happened. That was my mistake, and I don't plan on making it again."

"From what I saw, Sin handled himself pretty well. He seems to know what he's doing"

James' voice rose in frustration. "Sin doesn't have a investigator license. You're a lawyer, so you should know that it's illegal for people to run around interfering with an ongoing investigation."

"I'm an entertainment attorney, not a criminal one," she reminded him. "But this is about family."

"No, it's about me doing my job as you and Sin have reminded me *often*." James sighed. "But, after talking to Carla, I do want to check this out, so I've decided to drive to Salinas and check this name and address out."

"Yes!" Dana pumped her fist in the air. "But who do you think gave you the tip?"

"Carla suggested that considering the amount of the reward that's being offered for information, whoever it was will step forward when the time is right."

"That's probably true, and if this latest tip turns out to be a bust, then you can just pass the note on to Agent Conway."

"Thank you, Detective Mansfield. I'm sure he'll be more than pleased to get all of my discarded leads."

His teasing helped ease the tension that was building because of Sin. Dana gave him a kiss on the cheek.

"I'm glad that you like my suggestion and I've got another one more brilliant than that."

James lifted a cautious brow. "Oh really? You're not going to suggest that you go with me are you?"

"No, not to Salinas."

"Good."

"Just as far as Carmel.

"What?"

"Since you'll be headed to the Peninsula why don't I ride down with you. It'll be a nice ride, and I can do some shopping while I'm there."

James frowned. "I'm going on business, not on vacation."

"Yes, but if I go down with you we'll have a little more time together. Remember, I'll be heading for L.A. soon and I can leave from there." She upped the ante. "We could spend the night at a ritzy hotel together before I go."

James had no objection to that.

****

Sin was incensed. As he went about his work day, he only grew more agitated about Starr not sharing the information that was in that note.

By early afternoon he decided that he would jump in his car and head to Marin County. He was going to get the information he wanted from James Starr, and that was that. If the name and address on that paper would help solve this case, he would do what he had to do to get it.

He was walking to his car to start his trip to the Bay Area when his cell phone rang. It was Dana.

"Hi, what's up?" He didn't want to tell her that he was headed her way. She might warn Starr, but she had a surprise for him.

"James and I are about an hour from the Peninsula. He decided to come down that way today. He's in the convenience store right now picking up some snacks, so listen carefully because he'll be back in a minute. He'll be dropping me off in front of the Carmel shopping center on Ocean Avenue. After that he'll be headed to Salinas to check out the man named in the note."

"Okay, then give me the name and the address. I'll meet him there," Sin lied.

Dana wasn't fooled. "No, I think you'll try to do this on your own, and it could turn out to be a disaster. So, just follow him to Salinas from the shopping center and the two of you can have each other's backs when he gets to where he's going. That's the deal."

Sin had no choice but to accept the deal. Dana described the car that James was driving.

"Starr's not going to be happy. Why are you doing this?"

"Do you have to ask? Family first, and you're family."

CHAPTER 24

"I know what I'm doing, Ray. Don't worry."

Dana gave an exasperated sigh. Before leaving for the Peninsula, she stopped by the boat to change clothes, pack, and to let her sister and brother-in-law know where she was going. Bev was out on an errand, but Ray was there and, despite reservations, wished her the best.

"I know you do," Ray agreed, "And I know that James is a good guy. It's just that you've been through a lot, and deserve to be happy. I hope the two of you can make it."

His words brought tears to Dana's eyes. Ray was her friend long before he became her brother-in-law, and although they had disagreements over the years, the relationship between them remained strong. He was the type of man who knew what to say to friends to make them feel better. He also knew how to be diplomatic.

The same couldn't be said about Bev. Her sister had no reservations about expressing her opinion about whatever was happening in Dana's life. As her older sister, she was protective, and not always tactful.

The call from Bev came when Dana and James were only minutes from Carmel's main shopping district.

"I know you're a full grown woman, but I just want to make sure that your heart remains safely intact," Bev replied rolling her eyes at her husband who had warned her not to interfere with Dana's love life. "I saw how the two of you interacted when we were in New York."

"And?" Dana couldn't help but be curious about her sister's opinion, even though she tried to tell herself that she didn't care.

"And I liked what I saw. He seems kind and he's respectful, and I liked the way he looked at you."

"How was that?"

"As if you were the best thing that ever happened to him and you looked at him the same way."

"That's how you and Ray look at each other."

There was a pregnant pause on the other end before Bev responded. "I just want you to go into this with your eyes wide open."

"I appreciate that thought, but I'm much stronger than I've been in the past." The words *and not as needy* remained unsaid. "It's taken a while, but Sis, I'm really there."

Bev could hear the certainty in her sister's voice. "Okay, then that's all I want to know."

The ladies said their goodbyes just as James pulled up across the street from the Carmel Plaza Shopping Center. He found an empty parking space.

"So have I passed your sister's inspection?" James was pleased by Dana's end of the conversation. From what he could tell she defended their budding relationship against her sister's concern.

"You've passed my inspection," she told him. "That's the only one that matters." Dana leaned across the console and planted a kiss on his cheek. "Call me when you're on your way back to Carmel. I'll go on to the Inn and meet you there."

After getting out of the car she waited until he pulled away before starting across the street to the shopping center. Glancing surreptitiously up and down the street she tried to see if she could spot Sin's car. She couldn't, but she knew that he was around somewhere.

As she headed into the Plaza she thought about how a few years ago she never would have done something that the man in her life might not like. She had been a pleaser, anxious to do anything to keep a man in her life, even if it was to her detriment. How times had changed.

She doubted that James would be pleased with her having told Sin to follow him to Salinas, but she would deal with that later. She liked James a lot and could see a strong relationship evolving between them. If she made a mistake regarding her decision, she was willing to accept the responsibility, as well as the consequences.

****

Hardman would give it a week. If the information that he left in the mailbox in Tiburon didn't lead to the arrest of Robert Heflin then he would take care of the man himself. After that he was out of here. The longer he stayed in this country the more likely the chance would be of his bumping into someone who might recognize him. That couldn't happen.

All he could do was hope that he left the information in capable hands. There was no doubt that Darnell and Sinclair had hired the most competent person possible to investigate the abduction. He would trust their decision.

Hardman moved to the window that looked onto the streets of San Francisco. He hadn't planned on staying in the city by the Bay. His plan had been to drop the note off and return to the island, but he wanted to know the outcome of his endeavor. Plus, he was too wound up to travel. The past few days had left him practically giddy. The only thing that he could think about was having come face-to-face with his extremely handsome, exceptionally intelligent, and highly successful son.

He loved his daughter from the very depths of his heart, although he met her only once, and very briefly. Of course, she didn't know who he was. He never imagined that he would have another experience in his life that would mean as much to him as that single moment, but he was wrong. The time spent with Sinclair he would cherish until the day he died.

It was hard for him to believe that a man like him had fathered such wonderful children. Only one fact overshadowed his euphoria. He had no idea who Sinclair's mother might be.

Hardman never thought of himself as being sexually promiscuous, although he had to admit that in his youth his sexual appetite was voracious. Despite that, he was safe and used protection. Still, his son's existence couldn't be denied.

It never occurred to him that the day would come when he might need to recall any of his sexual liaisons before marrying Bev. Why would he? None of them meant anything to him.

When he was in Sinclair's office, he'd had a flicker of hope that his son might have a picture of his mother among the array of photographs on display. That didn't happen. Now he was left to guess who the woman might have been. In reviewing his past, Hardman assumed that he must have been in his teens when Sinclair was conceived. Unfortunately, he was especially mobile during those years, moving across the country trying to survive. Women of all ages had been plentiful then, and he indulged lavishly in their abundance. No matter how hard he tried, he couldn't come up with a name or the face of the woman who might have been Sinclair's mother.

Being a practical man, Hardman decided that there was no need to dwell on the matter. What was important was the fact that he had a daughter and he had a son. The kidnapping had hurt them both, and he was absolutely determined to get retribution from the people who harmed his children and grandchildren. He swore on his life that each of the abductors would pay.

CHAPTER 25

James wasn't aware of being followed until he was inside the Salinas city limits. He took an exit off the highway onto a street leading to the neighborhood in which Robert Heflin, the suspected abductor, was suppose to reside. When he glanced in his rear-view mirror he saw that a car he'd noticed on the highway was still behind him.

It didn't take him long to figure out who was driving the vehicle. He doubted that his newly acquired house was bugged by the FBI, which meant nobody in that agency would be aware of his destination. There was the possibility that the anonymous note writer could have set him up and was following him, but he doubted it. That left one other possibility.

Making it obvious to his stalker that he had been spotted, James pulled into a supermarket parking lot and waited. When Sin got out of his car and started walking toward him, James could feel his heart constrict. That one possibility had become a reality. Dana betrayed him.

Sin knew that he had been discovered. As he approached Starr's automobile, he didn't intend to apologize. Starr knew what Sin wanted. Either he would comply or he could expect for Sin to be his permanent shadow until the case was solved. Peering at him through the passenger window, Sin saw Starr slip a digital recorder into his jacket pocket before he unlocked the door. Sin slid in beside him.

"I'm not going away," he warned.

James was perturbed. "I figured that."

"So why the recorder? Do you plan on recording me strong arming you into taking me with you?"

James snickered. "Man, you are something else. You know that you need a license to do this."

"That's already been established, but if you'll remember, when I went with you before I signed a legal waiver releasing your company from liability."

James blew out a frustrated breath. "Man, this is *not* reality television. It can be dangerous. You have a family!"

"You did too, at one time, and how long did it take you to lose your thirst for revenge?" Sin held his eyes.

James didn't respond. Both he and Sin knew the answer to that question. They were men whose values were honed in the streets. There were codes by which they lived then and now. Anybody who touched family members would pay a price. Nothing more needed to be said.

Sin listened quietly as James explained how he planned on handling this latest effort. He would use one of the many false identities that he adopted as an investigator to go straight to the front door of the suspect's house.

"I'll be posing as an insurance agent doing a claims call, and I just happen to be showing up at the wrong address."

"You mean to tell me that whoever is inside that house is going to open their door to a 6' 6", bald black man with an earring in his ear?" Sin scoffed. "That's hard to believe. Even I wouldn't do that. I hate to tell you this, man, but you look menacing."

"Maybe so, but you'd be surprised at how charming I can be."

Sin rolled his eyes. "Hell, ain't that much charm in the world."

"Okay, smart aleck, but you'd be shocked at how helpful people can be to a lost stranger."

"No wonder there's so much rampant crime," Sin deadpanned.

They arrived at the house of the man who had been named in the note as the third abductor. This house was much different than the one in Inglewood. It was a neat, well kept bungalow in a quiet, middle class neighborhood.

To make his story sound credible, James drove around the block to get the name of a street so that he could identify it as his intended destination. The plan was for Sin to remain in the car while James made initial contact. They developed a prearranged signal that James would use if he needed assistance.

Sin wanted to be at the front door as well to make sure that his former nemesis gathered all of the information needed, but, he waited. He was willing to give James the chance to prove himself. If he failed, Sin was ready to take over whether Starr liked it or not.

He was waiting and watching when his cell phone rang. It was Nedra. He let it go to voice mail. He would return her call later. He certainly didn't want her to know what he was doing. The last time they talked, his wife made it clear how she felt about his investigative efforts.

"If you get arrested, I'm not going to bail you out," she warned. "If you get hurt, you're going to wish you were dead when I get through with you. God forbid that anything worse happens, because I'll never forgive you."

She told him that she was bringing the children home. "Not only because we miss you, but I need to keep an eye on you before you do something crazy."

Unfortunately, she was too late. If "something crazy" went down today Sin planned on being right in the middle it.

A woman, responded to the doorbell that James rang. She was understandably cautious seeing the tall stranger standing at her front door. She kept the storm door between them securely locked.

A smiling James introduced himself and held up his phony ID. He inquired about the fictitious person for whom he was supposedly searching. As expected, her answer was negative. He proceeded to go into his desperately confused act, successfully soliciting her sympathy as well as the information that he was seeking.

"I'm sorry, but nobody lives here but me. My son, Robert, recently moved out into a place of his own."

The first name was right, but just in case—

"Oh, I'm sorry, Mrs..."

"Heflin," she confirmed.

"So, your son doesn't work at Rosewood Industries?"

"No, he works for Tech Play in Carmel. He's in computers. He just got a promotion," she told him proudly.

James feigned pleasant surprise. "Oh really? I live in Carmel, but I've never heard of Tech Play. Where is it located?"

She provided the address and a detailed description of the building. "He's been working there for years. My son's a wiz when it comes to computers."

"So is mine," James said brightly. "He's kind of shy though because he speaks with a slight lisp."

"Oh my goodness!" she exclaimed. "It's the same with my son. He's got a lisp, but I keep telling him that it's hardly noticeable."

They commiserated over their common dilemma until James decided that he had enough information. He apologized for coming to the wrong house, thanked her for her time and trouble, and returned to the car. Sin couldn't tell by his stoic expression if the visit had been successful.

"What's up?" he asked eagerly.

"I think I hit pay dirt."

Starr reached into his pocket and handed him the recorder that Sin spotted previously. Starting the car, James flashed him a wily smile before pulling away.

"So what is this about?" Sin indicated the recorder.

"It's a copy of that telephone call from the kidnapper. I was listening to it on my way here. Play it."

Doing as instructed, Sin tensed as the voice of the abductor who called Dana filled the vehicle. The recording lasted under a minute, but it felt longer. When it was over, he turned to James.

"Okay, so what?"

Having driven out of the Heflin's neighborhood, James pulled over to the side of the road and parked. "Play it again and listen carefully to every word that's said."

Once again Sin complied. In an attempt to disguise the voice it was electronically distorted, but the words were spoken clearly, except—

Frowning, Sin played the recording again and again and again. When it ended the last time he turned to James.

"It's subtle but it sounds like he's got a lisp."

James met Sin's eyes and smiled.

****

210

Dana made her rounds of the stores in the Plaza making various purchases. Among them was a sexy pair of underwear that she planned on donning this evening. She was sure that James would enjoy removing them.

She wondered how his efforts were going. There was little doubt that he would resent her having conspired with Sin to follow him, but hopefully she and James could get past that. Sin and he made a good team. If his presence turned out to be an advantage for James maybe he would forgive her deception. All she could do was hope.

CHAPTER 26

"His name is Robert Heflin," Sin said into his cell phone. "And he works for Tech Play in Carmel."

James sat listening to his end of the conversation. He had to admit that Sin was turning out to be an asset to this investigation. Sin's daughter and niece had identified the still comatose Andy Vegas as the man who picked them up at school. The disguise he wore at the time didn't fool them. Like James, Sin was keeping up with the FBI's interrogation of Jack Spencer. The authorities still couldn't prove that he was involved in the abduction, since he wasn't talking. To further detain him, Spencer was being held for a slew of unpaid parking tickets while the kidnapping investigation continued.

When James was in New York taking care of arrangements for Nate, he had turned Spencer's background check over to one of his employees. The information gathering was thorough, but somehow Sin had assembled additional facts that he shared with both the authorities and with James' agency.

Sin wouldn't say where he got his information. When questioned his answer was always the same, "contacts." While the identification of those other contacts might be a mystery, the one he was talking to presently wasn't. Media mogul, Brandon Plaine, was one of the most influential men on the Peninsula, and he was Sin's best friend. His power, empathy and friendship with Sinclair Reasoner, made him an invaluable resource.

After a series of answering yes and no, Sin jotted down some notes. Disconnecting, he turned to James with a wide grin.

James lifted an inquisitive brow. "What's up?"

"Brandon has heard of Tech Play. It's a mid-sized company with customers throughout the Peninsula, and one of those customers is the school that Gillian and Nia attend. The company installed the computer system and provides maintenance services."

James returned Sin's grin. "Heflin might have gotten the information about the girls' schedules straight off the school computers."

Sin nodded. " *And,* Tech Play is located in a building that Brandon owns."

James chuckled. "This gets better and better."

"There's more. Follow me to my house and there should be a job application waiting for you on my computer. You can start work as a custodian in the building where Robert Heflin works tomorrow."

James rubbed his hands together eagerly. The job would give him full access to every office in the building, including the suspect's.

Sin continued. "Once inside, see what you can find on Heflin. Meanwhile, Brandon will do some research and find out what he can. If Heflin turns out to be a viable suspect, Brandon agrees with you that his name should go to the authorities."

"As opposed to you beating him to death," James quipped good-naturedly.

"It's an alternative." Sin didn't crack a smile. "Do you want to get inside or not?"

"I definitely want to get inside."

James was ecstatic. It seemed that the anonymous tipster might have handed him a pot of gold. But, Sin wasn't finished with the good news.

"Brandon wants an exclusive interview with you if what you find from your investigation leads to Heflin's arrest."

James stilled. "I see, but I want to be certain about what you're telling me. If I nab this creep, my company will receive the publicity for the effort."

"Yes."

"Agent Conway won't be pleased. This case is a big one for the Bureau."

"If the Bureau solves the case first, then they get the publicity. But my bet is on you."

Although he remained stoic, James was pleased by Sin's words of confidence. He was really beginning to like this guy.

As he followed Sin's car back to his house in Carmel-by-the Sea, he thought about Sin's presence in Salinas. It hadn't turned out to be the detriment that he originally thought it might be. However, Sin hadn't been thrilled with the investigative process. It seemed that the life of a P.I. wasn't for him.

"I didn't like staying in the car," Sin told him. "It was boring."

"That's pretty much what a Private Investigator does," James answered honestly. "It's mostly observation, research and conducting interviews."

"Oh, I hoped that the job would be more exciting," Sin grumbled, looking disappointed.

When they reached the Reasoner house, the job application was waiting. While James filled it out with the fictitious information that he would use to create his persona, Sin cooked dinner. It turned out to be delicious.

"Man, you really know your way around a kitchen." James was surprised

"I'm the one who does the cooking around here when our housekeeper is off."

"You mean that fine wife of yours doesn't cook?"

"Nope, she warms up and brings home carry out." Sin cleared the table. "But what she lacks in culinary skills she makes up for it in other ways."

"You seem happy."

"That's an understatement. I don't know what I did in my life to deserve Nedra or our kids, but whatever it was I am grateful every day." He paused, and added pointedly. "The women in the Stillwaters family are special. They know how to cast a spell on a man. Ask Ray, he knows."

James didn't have to ask anybody. He already knew, and that's what hurt so badly about Dana's betrayal. Meeting her had made him feel like life might have given him another chance at love, but now he wasn't sure.

Sin seemed to read James' mind. Placing the dishes in the dishwasher, he went back to the table and addressed a brooding James.

"Dana is a good woman, Starr…"

"Don't," James warned.

Sin held his hands up in a gesture of surrender. "I'm just saying."

Sin backed down, knowing that at least he tried to help mend any broken fences between James and Dana. She had made a decision to help him, and he felt obligated to return the favor. What happened between the two of them was out of his hands.

"Do you need a place to stay tonight?" He assumed that James wouldn't be staying with Dana this evening.

"No, I'm cool. I'd better get going if I'm going to report to work tomorrow."

Sin escorted him to the front door and bid him good evening, with a warning. "I'm putting you on notice; Starr, I want this thing wrapped up as quickly as possible."

"Patience isn't one of your strong points, is it?"

Sin was blunt. "No, it's not."

CHAPTER 27

"No, everything is fine," Dana reassured her sister as she sat in the Inn waiting to hear from James.

"If you say so." Bev didn't sound convinced. "How are things going down there? Since you're not staying there, have you checked on my daughter's house? Are those paparazzi still slithering in the bushes?"

"Careful, Sis, your contempt for honest, hard working snakes is showing."

Bev sniggered. "That's a good one."

"But seriously, everything is fine." And it was, as far as Dana knew. She didn't want to tell her that she hadn't been by the Stewart home as she indicated she would before she left Tiburon. "Security is checking on the house regularly."

She figured this was true since that was their job. If time allowed, she would stop by the place tomorrow before leaving for home.

Bev's next inquiry caught her by surprise. "How is James doing? Has he followed up on whatever it is he's doing down there?"

Dana hesitated. Was Bev asking the question because James wouldn't offer specifics when Ray asked why he was returning to the Peninsula so suddenly? Or, had Bev sensed in her voice that there might be trouble between her and James?

Just as she was about to answer, her cell phone indicated another call. She said goodbye to Bev and answered the call.

"Dana."

The sound of James' voice made her heart race. She hoped that he would call, but she wasn't sure if her actions had put an end to what might have been. She responded with a hushed, "Yes."

James drew a jagged breath. Simply hearing Dana's voice made him want her, but his response gave no hint of his conflicting emotions.

"I've rented a hotel room for the night. I think that we need to take a break for a while."

His words hurt. "If that's the way you feel, I have to respect that. Maybe in your opinion what I did by contacting Sin wasn't the right thing to do, but it's done and I'm not going to offer any excuses."

James liked the fact that she didn't make any excuses, but it didn't ease the pain of her betrayal. "I'll be staying here, on the Peninsula, for a while on the job before returning to the Bay Area. Will you still be flying back to L.A. tomorrow?"

"That's the plan."

There was silence on the other end. Dana knew he was pondering what to say as his parting words.

"You know, Dana, honesty is the foundation of any good relationship."

"So is love," she replied.

"I have a question for you."

"What?"

"Will your family always control your actions?" There was bitterness in his voice.

"I'm the only one who controls my actions, and it's taken a long time for me to get to this point." Dana took an exasperated breath. "I apologize for deceiving you, James, and I hope you will accept my apology. As for my family,

Nia and Gillian were innocent victims of a crime and I want the people responsible caught."

"I thought that was why I was hired," James reminded her. "You don't trust me to see that this job is done?"

"I trust you, but I'll do what I have to do to make sure that justice is served." With those words she said goodbye.

As soon as they disconnected Dana began to miss him, but crying about it wasn't on the agenda. She had shed her last tears over a man. A long time ago, she vowed that any tears shed over a relationship in the future would be ones of joy.

A short time later, Sinclair called.

"How are you doing?"

"I've been better," she admitted.

"I'm really sorry if this cost you."

"I had an idea what could happen when I called you, but if this Heflin guy is guilty of kidnapping the girls it will be worth it."

He filled her in on what occurred after he followed James. Dana was anxious.

"Do you think James will be in any danger going into Tech Play undercover?"

"It's a computer company, Dana, not mafia headquarters. Anyway, Starr has been in this game for a long time. He's still standing. He knows what he's doing."

"You're right."

"And Dana, from what I can tell from his personality, Starr seems to be the kind of guy who will stew for a while when he's angry, but I think that he'll eventually come around. He seems to really like you. He's too smart to let a good thing go."

"Thanks, Sin." His words made her feel better. All she could do was hope that they were true.

****

Sitting in the break room at his new "job", James thought about how others were making his real job easy. He had been an employee for less than eight hours and had gathered so much information about Heflin that he could literally see the noose being placed around the man's neck. It turned out that James' supervisor was a certified, card carrying gossip.

His name was Dan Santos, a rail thin man in his late fifties who had been employed as the maintenance supervisor for fifteen years. There wasn't a person who worked in the building that he didn't know, and whose business he wouldn't reveal. As he trained James for his new position, he filled him in on who was married, divorced or single and who was sleeping with whom. By mid-morning James' head was spinning with all of the intimate details about the lives of people he didn't know.

Dan talked nonstop. Most of what he said was of no value, but after too many hours of listening to his mindless chatter James' patience finally paid off. When they reached the floor occupied by Tech Play, there he was. The man James was looking for was sitting at his desk in one of the offices.

Robert Heflin was an average looking man of average height, weight and stature. He wasn't as old as James assumed. He appeared to be in his mid-thirties, with dark brown hair, cut to precision, hazel eyes beneath bushy eyebrows, and a solemn expression. He looked nothing like the sinister ring leader of a gang of ruthless kidnappers. Most people would never suspect him of breaking the law, but James knew that most of the criminals he'd met were average looking people, just like Heflin.

Dan confirmed Heflin's identity by introducing him to James. Heflin looked at James from behind a pair of stylish reading glasses and his solemn expression quickly transformed into a welcoming smile. Reaching across the desk he shook hands with James, greeting him warmly.

"Nice meeting you."

Heflin's eye contact was direct. His grip was strong and his greeting seemed sincere. If James had met him under any other circumstances, he might have liked the man.

"You've got a great place here," James complimented, looking around at the well furnished office.

"Yes, it's comfortable," Heflin replied. Anxious to get back to work, he resumed reading.

Leaving the office, James was satisfied. Not only did he have a face to go with the name, but when Heflin greeted him James was pleased with what he heard. As slight as it was, one word was off kilter. The man did have a lisp.

James was able to fill in some of the blanks about Heflin when Dan and he were in the cafeteria during their break. He didn't have to fish hard for information, all James had to do was toss out the line.

"I really think that I'm going to enjoy working here," he told Dan. "Everybody seems to be nice, especially that Heflin guy up at Tech Play. He was real friendly."

"Yeah, he is," Dan agreed, "and those supervisors of his keep him practically chained to his desk. The man's a workaholic. He's usually the first one to come into this building in the morning and the last one to leave at night. He lives and breathes computers."

James tried to sound empathetic. "Does he ever take a vacation?"

"As a matter of fact he just came back from one not that long ago. He was gone for three weeks. That's the longest I've seen him take off since he's been working at Tech Play."

Dan went on to tell James everything that he knew about Heflin except the color of his boxer shorts. It seemed that he was well respected by his colleagues, and long overdue for the promotion that he received. As for his personal life, Dan told him that Heflin was recently divorced. He and his ex-wife were childless, but she was awarded the house and a substantial financial settlement.

"The poor guy had to move in with his mother for a while to regroup." Dan shook his head in sympathy. Lifting an interested brow, he was ready to gather information on James. "You married?"

"Divorced," he answered truthfully.

"Then you know what I'm saying about these women taking a man to the cleaners in divorce court. I'm telling you, that woman Rob was married to…"

James listened to the picture that Dan was painting. It seemed that Heflin was a man embittered by a divorce, and he was in need of money. While his observation of Heflin was brief, James had formed some first impressions.

Heflin's office was extremely neat, indicating that he was well organized. He liked being in control. Having all of his bases covered was probably important to him.

If that was the case, it was a certainty that Heflin was the one who planned the abduction. James would bet his recently inherited fortune that never in Heflin's wildest dreams would he and his merry band of men have factored into the equation that their kidnap plan would be thwarted by a keg of dynamite named Gillian Reasoner.

It must have been a shock when they opened the door to that little room the girls were suppose to be in only to find it empty. He would have paid anything to have seen their faces when the three of them realized that their dreams of instant wealth had turned to dust.

Whatever Heflin's plans were if the kidnapping had been successful, they were now irrelevant. James was here to see to it that the only plan in Robert Heflin's future would be a long prison sentence.

CHAPTER 28

James had barely clocked out of his first day on the job before Sin called to get an update. He wanted to meet with him for dinner in Carmel. James agreed.

The restaurant where they met was located in a courtyard off of Ocean Avenue. Being in the area again reminded him of Dana, and what caused the rift between them. After talking to her last night he stopped himself a dozen times from picking up the telephone, calling her back, and telling her that he made a mistake—but, he didn't. He couldn't trust her. That bridge was too long to cross.

Sin was waiting at a table on the restaurant's patio. He was anxious to learn what happened at Tech Play. Over dinner, James filled him in.

"You're telling me that Heflin just happened to be on vacation during the same time that the girls were snatched," Sin noted eagerly.

"He was probably the one who was supposed to pick up the money at the drop," James speculated. "The authorities know that Spencer wasn't off work. He showed up every day to patrol your neighborhood. That means that he was hiding in plain sight, reporting to his buddies what was happening behind those gates."

"And your guy reported that Andy Vega was on a so-called vacation too, during that time, giving him ample opportunity to pull off the kidnapping."

"Right," James affirmed. "And now that the girls have identified Vega, his fate is sealed. If he ever awakes up from the coma, he'd better find a good attorney."

Sin wasn't pacified. His eyes glazed over in anger.

"Vega drugged my daughter and niece, and left them in that tiny room…"

"He was the one who did the actual dirty work," James agreed, but hoping to quell Sin's rising rage, he added, "Yet Gillian out smarted all three of them, and spoiled their little party. I can't imagine how proud you and your wife must be."

His words had the intended effect. At the mention of his child's heroics, Sin relaxed.

"We are proud." His manner softened. "What's next?"

"I'll turn the information I've gathered on Heflin over to Agent Conway. I think that there's enough to hang him."

James released a relieved breath when Sin nodded in agreement. He was aware that Sin still wanted revenge, but they both knew that there was a fine line between impeding the investigation and assisting with it. Neither wanted to jeopardize the case against the abductors.

"Vega got what he deserved, Sin. If he lives he'll never be the same again. Let the courts take care of the other two. When I go back tomorrow, I'll see if I can get anything more on Heflin. I should be able to wrap this up after that."

"No argument there. It'll be interesting to see what Jack Spencer will have to say when he hears Heflin's name, especially since he claims not to know Andy Vega." It was Brandon Plaine's research that uncovered the fact that Spencer and Vega attended the same high school. "My only hope is that Brandon can dig up a connection between Heflin, Vega and Spencer."

Sin's cell phone vibrated. He glanced at caller I.D. and then looked at James.

"I'll get it later." He started to put the phone away. James stayed his hand.

"I can tell by the look on your face that call is from Dana. It's all right, answer it. She deserves to know what's happening."

Sin greeted her with a smile in his voice. "How's it going?"

"I've been anxious all day!" Dana exclaimed. "It's been a long one."

She had taken a flight back to Los Angeles yesterday and went straight to the new condo that she hadn't stepped foot in for nearly a month. When she walked into the spacious living room with its towering ceilings, the place smelled stale. The curtains were drawn and the interior looked dreary. Boxes were everywhere. There was barely any food in her refrigerator, and only one bottle of water. In her bedroom, the bed remained unmade. It had been since the day of the kidnapping. Tossing her travel bag and purse aside, Dana crawled into bed fully dressed. She didn't care. She was too depressed.

"That's what caring about someone will do for you," she lamented pulling the cover over her head. But, she vowed not to stay that way.

This morning she felt better. Donning the sexy new underwear that she bought in Carmel, she covered it with a new dress that she also purchased, and slipped into a pair of new shoes. Feeling like a new woman, she strutted into her law office with the confidence of a queen.

The rest of the day was spent playing catch up on work and fending off media calls that were still coming. It was those inquiries that wouldn't let her forget the danger that

James might be in . Despite her efforts to ignore the feeling of disquiet that plagued her, she finally succumbed to her curiosity and called Sin.

Dispensing with small talk, she got straight to the point. "What happened with James and Heflin today?"

Dana listened intently as Sin recounted what James had told him about the day's events.

"Contacting the FBI will be the next step," he concluded.

"That sounds like a good idea," she agreed. "Does James think that Heflin is the one who beat Vega so badly?"

"I don't know. Why don't you ask him?"

James started, unexpectedly, when Sin thrust the cell phone in his hand. Excusing himself to go to the men's room, he was gone before James could utter a protest.

Dana's mouth went dry at this unexpected development. She would murder Sinclair Reasoner when she saw him. She had no idea he was with James.

Taking a fortifying breath to steady her emotions, Dana told herself that this really wasn't a big deal. James and she weren't adversaries. He did work for her family.

"Hello, James." Her tone was crisp and professional. "How are you?"

"I'm fine, Dana." His tone was crisp and professional as well.

"I have a question for you." She proceeded to ask him the same one that she had asked Sin.

"I can only assume that it was Heflin who beat Vega. He didn't want him to talk," James replied.

"He could have solved that by simply killing him" Dana countered. "Maybe they quarreled about something and had a fight."

"What we saw in that house was more than a simple fight. Vega was tortured. Whatever the case, Heflin is probably on pins and needles hoping that Spencer won't talk."

If they were on good terms, he might have discussed the case further. James valued her opinion, and enjoyed the lively discussions that they used to have. Instead there was an awkward silence full of empty spaces that needed to be filled, but weren't. Dana finally responded.

"Thank you for the info" She couldn't think of anything else to say.

"You're welcome." James manner was as cool as Dana's. If that's the way she wanted it, that's the way it would be.

The goodbyes were brisk. The call was disconnected, and the gulf between them widened.

****

"How close do you think he is to wrapping this thing up?" Bev asked her sister as she and Ray sat on the upper deck of their houseboat talking to her on speaker phone. Dana had called them with an update on the investigation. She gave no specifics.

"It's going well," she informed them. "James has a solid lead on a suspect that he's working on now. Hopefully, everybody involved in the kidnapping will be in custody soon."

"Have you called Darnell and Thad and told them?" asked Bev.

"I called, but I got voice mail. I left a message for them to contact me."

"Has James had any word on how Vega is doing?" Ray hadn't been able to get the sight of the man's battered body out of his mind.

"He's still in critical condition. The hospital said he'll be a vegetable if he ever wakes up."

Ray tuned out the rest of the conversation as his mind drifted back to that day, and the house in Inglewood. Not only was it the brutality of the beating that haunted him, but he kept remembering the stranger who drove pass him when he was sitting in the car waiting for the others.

The moment their eyes met was brief. It should have been forgotten, but there was something about the moment that bothered him. It was those eyes. Ray couldn't forget them. What he saw in those eyes haunted him, but he couldn't pinpoint the reason why.

CHAPTER 29

It had been three days since Dana spoke to James regarding Heflin, and those days were excruciating. She didn't want to miss him, but she did. She didn't want to worry about him and the work he was doing in Carmel, but she did.

After the stunt that Sin pulled putting James on his cell phone, Dana was upset with him. She was giving him the silent treatment for now, but she knew that eventually she would forgive him. As for her sister, she didn't want Bev to know that James and she had a tiff. That would only lead to a lecture from Bev about Dana's dysfunctional love life. She didn't want to hear it.

Dana avoided talking to Ray as well. He would mention any concern that she might have about James to Bev, which would prompt a call to Dana to find out what was going on. It seemed that she just couldn't win.

Darnell turned out to be a recurring source of information for Dana. Like her brother, the capture of the abductors had become an obsession. But, this time when she called to talk to Dana there was something else on her niece's mind.

"Thad's not sure we'll be able to move back home to Carmel when this is over," she told her aunt. "He thinks that after what happened we may not be safe, and have peace of mind again. But, I told him we're going home, come hell or high water."

Dana could understand how she felt. Before the kidnapping, the celebrity couple lived an idyllic life on the quiet cul-de-sac in Carmel. They were enjoying peace and serenity far from Hollywood.

Presently, they were visiting Darnell's in-laws in Michigan, dodging the media and hiding from the paparazzi. A single photo of their little family could earn a photographer a year's income. With that at stake, Thad might be right. It would take time for their lives to get back to normal. Despite that, Dana tried to be encouraging.

"Home is wherever you, Thad and Nia make it. The bond between you and Thad is strong, and I know that you'll weather this storm no matter where you are."

There was a pause on the line, which meant that Darnell was thinking. That wasn't always a good thing

"You know something, Auntie, you're right! Wherever we are is home, and when the time is right, we're going *back* to our house!" Darnell declared. "And just listen to you," Darnell teased. "You're beginning to wax poetic since you met James Starr."

Dana became defensive. "What do you mean by that?"

Did her niece know what was happening between James and her? Had somebody talked? More than likely it was Sin. There was entirely too much communication in this family.

Darnell dismissed her reaction. "It was just a comment. I spoke to James yesterday and he said that things were coming along smoothly with his investigation of that Heflin guy."

"Oh really?" Dana tried not to sound too interested in hearing about James, but couldn't quite pull it off.

"Yes, *really*." There was a tinge of amusement in Darnell's voice. Dana stiffened.

"I assume that part of your conversation happened to include my personal life."

"Uh, no." Plain spoken as always, Darnell emitted an indulgent sigh. "Aunt Dana, if there's something between you and James Starr, I wish you well. But to be frank, right now my priorities have nothing to do with your love life." She went on to inform Dana that the FBI would be taking Helfin in as a person of interest the next day. "And I got *that* first hand, from Agent Conway," she finished.

"That's surprising. The FBI is usually tight-lipped about suspects and making arrest."

Darnell snickered. "Let's just say that I used special persuasion to get the information. And after Heflin is brought in, Carla will continue to handle the media. We'll issue another statement thanking the FBI for assisting in the capture. Of course Webb Starr will be given special credit."

Dana was pleased by that news. After this case was solved, James' company would be in high demand.

"When the news breaks about the arrest, the media will probably start hounding you again," Darnell warned. "Are you going to stay in L.A.?"

"Yes, and the media is still snooping around anyway, but I direct all questions to our spokesperson."

"Well, if you need a break, our house in Carmel is always available. Although I'm not quite sure that it will be much of a refuge when the FBI releases its statement. We're winding up our vacation with Thad's parents and heading back to Stillwaters for a while. We won't be around when things heat up again. Hopefully, it won't take too long for this whole thing to die down."

"I hope not, and thanks for the invitation to Carmel."

Dana knew that she probably wouldn't be going to the Peninsula as long as James was there. Yet, it was nice of

Darnell to offer. It was also good to find out that James remained safe on his assignment.

****

"I want to be there when they bring Heflin out," Sinclair Reasoner insisted as he and James strolled along the beach.

After his stint at his pretend job, James stopped by the cul-de-sac to dispense some paperwork to his employees who were on duty. Sin was headed to the beach for a walk and invited him to come along.

James' undercover stint was coming to an end. The FBI was ready to apprehend Heflin. Sin wanted to know the details.

James was evasive. "They have their own timetable and way of doing things. I don't know exactly what time tomorrow that they'll make their move."

"Well, I'll park near the building and wait."

James groaned in exasperation. Sin Reasoner could really be obstinate. He reminded him of—

James shook his head, forcing thoughts of Dana out of his head. It had been a long time since any woman occupied his thoughts so completely.

"Starr! Starr?"

James snapped out of his trance. "Uh, sorry. What did you say?"

"I was asking if you were going to be there tomorrow when they nab him, but it looks like your mind is a million miles away."

"Yes, I'm going to work tomorrow. I want to be there when everything goes down."

"So you can have that pleasure, but I can't," Sin groused.

James wasn't sympathetic. "That's the way of the world, my man."

They continued walking along the water's edge. The rhythm of the tide proved soothing for both men. Over the past few weeks they had been through a lot together. Now it looked as though their common goal might finally be achieved.

James was relieved. He had been under tremendous pressure and wasn't sure how much longer he could keep up the pace. His attempt to come to terms with Nate's death was as overwhelming as the responsibility of carrying on a growing business without him. Then there was this thing between him and Dana.

He had to admit that everything in his life changed dramatically from the moment he walked into her office. In a short span of time, he experienced emotions that he hadn't been sure he could feel again for a woman. If that wasn't unexpected enough, another change occurred that he once thought impossible—he was beginning to like Sinclair Reasoner.

"Has it ever crossed your mind how strange this is?" he asked Sin. "Here we are, two ex-gang members who once vowed to kill each other on sight, strolling peacefully along a California beach."

Sin chuckled. "Yes, it did cross my mind. But believe me, I'm a living witness to the fact that strange things do happen. You'd never believe some of the crazy twists and turns that my life has taken. I might share them with you sometime." He stooped to pick up a piece of drift wood and flung it into the ocean. "But my wife is an ordained minister and she says that there is a divine plan for everything."

James wasn't a religious man, but who was he to argue. "Do you believe that?"

"I've fought the idea of divine anything for years; but, after some of the experiences I've had while I've been with Nedra, I can't totally discount it."

James understood. After some of the things that happened in his own life, good and bad, he couldn't discount it either.

****

"Damn it!"

Hardman was frustrated. What was happening? He practically hand delivered Robert Heflin to that guy named Starr in Tiburon and the prick hadn't been picked up yet! What kind of investigator was Starr?

Hardman paced the room restlessly. He wanted to know what was happening, but didn't dare risk another trip to the Peninsula. Sinclair knew what he looked like, and he wasn't sure how he could explain or handle running into him again.

His son was smart. There was no doubt that he might become suspicious of a stranger popping up so often. It was difficult, but he would have to be patient.

Hardman decided to wait another day or two. If Heflin wasn't arrested by then, he would save the state of California the expense of holding a trial.

CHAPTER 30

You didn't have to pick me up," Dana insisted as she and Sin drove out of the airport terminal headed for Darnell and Thad's house. She was surprised to see him waiting for her.

"I didn't have anything else to do, and Darnell told me what time you were landing. I told Bev I'd come and get you."

Dana wanted to kick herself for coming to the Peninsula. Since Ray was in L.A. on business, Bev made plans to go to Carmel for the weekend and implored her sister to meet her there.

"We can spend some time together," she added as an incentive. "We haven't done that in such a long time. I'm staying at Darnell and Thad's house. We can just lie around and enjoy each other's company."

Dana tried to persuade her to substitute Carmel-by-the-Sea with Santa Barbara, but Bev was insistent. Dana didn't want to tell her that as long as James was on the Peninsula she didn't want to be caught dead in the area. She didn't want to take the chance of bumping into him.

The plan was to decline her sister's invitation using work as an excuse. But, she altered that plan after Sin called and provided her with an update on the investigation. Initially, Dana's manner toward him was cool.

"I'm still upset with you and that stunt you pulled with the cell phone."

"Sorry," he said without a sign of contrition. "But things are wrapping up with the investigation and James is headed back to Tiburon."

It was those words that helped her make the decision to spend the weekend with Bev.

As she drove along the highway, Dana wanted to treat Sin with indifference, but her anger toward him had fizzled. The man did nothing more than try to help her. There was no reason to hold on to resentment. Her thoughts turned elsewhere.

"Have the Feds taken Heflin in yet?"

"They hadn't earlier when I checked. We'll ride by the building and find out what's happening. I want to see the man who kidnapped Gillian and Nia marched out of the building in handcuffs—that is if we haven't missed it already."

"I certainly hope not." Dana was anxious to see the culprit as well. She wanted the man who planned the abduction to get what he deserved.

When they pulled onto the street where Tech Play's building was located, they were met by an array of police cars blocking their way. The area was cordoned off.

"What's going on?" Dana wondered aloud. "Let's go see."

Sin found the first available parking space and the two of them walked toward the building. As they neared it, Sin questioned an officer who was directing the growing crowd of curious gawkers.

"What's happening?"

"There's trouble ahead," the officer answered sternly.

"What kind of trouble?" Sin persisted.

"Can't say." He waved them on.

"I heard on my car radio that there's a hostage situation in there," someone said over Sin's shoulder. The stranger nodded toward a building.

Sin turned to Dana. "That's where Tech Play is located."

"Do you think that it has something to do with Heflin?" Dana wasn't sure if that was good or bad.

Sin withdrew his cell phone as they continued to move closer to the building. He dialed James' number. His voicemail answered.

"Who are you calling? Agent Conway?"

"I'm calling Starr, but he's not answering."

Startled, Dana drew back. "James? Why are you calling him? You said that he's in Tiburon."

"No, I said that he's headed back to Tiburon."

Dana stopped walking. Sin was ten steps ahead of her before he noticed. Turning, he saw her standing in the middle of the sidewalk, arms tightly folded. She was staring daggers at him.

"You lied," she spat. "Where is James?"

Sin nodded toward the Tech Play building.

"He's in there."

****

James was pissed. He definitely misread Robert Heflin. Having observed the man he didn't peg the mild mannered computer geek as threatening or dangerous. He was wrong.

From his position on the office floor where he had been forced to sit, James glanced up at Heflin. He was leaning against a desk pointing a gun at James and three other hostages. The weapon had been wrestled from one of the men he was holding—a FBI agent who came to escort him out of the building. James deduced that any promotion that the agent was expecting after this fiasco was gone. The guy barely got the chance to try and cuff Heflin before he found himself staring down the barrel of his own gun, or that's what one of the other hostages told him. James hadn't witnessed the incident.

He was watching from an upstairs window when the Feds pulled up to the building. Knowing what was about to happen, he made his way down to the Tech Play offices on the pretense of doing some cleaning. He wanted to be a witness to Heflin being taken into custody.

Nearly all of the employees had gone home for the day, but as usual Heflin was among the last employees to leave. James busied himself in an area near the suspect's office when the two agents entered. He heard the commotion, but by the time he stepped into the central reception area it was too late. Heflin had one of the officers in a chokehold with a gun pointed at his head. The officer who accompanied him was standing with his hands up.

Patty, a Tech Play employee who was working late, was taken as hostage along with James. That made four people who the computer whiz, turned abductor, could use as bargaining chips, but James saw the futility in the man's effort. There was no way that the FBI would let Heflin walk out of here a free man after holding two of their agents. Heflin was a smart man. He had to know that he would be lucky to walk out of the building alive. The sharpshooters were probably on the roof waiting for a good shot right now.

James looked from Heflin to his fellow captives. Patty had been sobbing hysterically, but she now sat quietly in wide-eyed shock.

One of the agents was trying to engage Heflin in conversation, a tactic that he probably learned in hostage negotiation class. The other agent kept eyeing one of the two guns in Heflin's possession. While one of the weapons was in Heflin's hand, the other one was lying on the desk beside him. That gun belonged to the second officer who was forced to relinquish it when his partner was threatened. James could almost see the wheels spinning in the agent's head as he was thinking of ways to get to the weapon. If he failed he risked putting all of their lives in jeopardy.

James stole a glance at Heflin. His demeanor worried him. Despite the dire situation, Heflin seemed a little too calm. James didn't like that. Any normal person in his position would be as nervous as hell.

Earlier, Heflin was ranting about being railroaded by a system that favors the rich and famous over the average citizen. He swore that he would die before he'd let the authorities put him in jail.

Presently, he was subdued. Leaning against his desk, holding a gun on his hostages, Heflin's eyes were blank. He was ignoring the chattering agent, looking pass him, staring into space.

A professional negotiator had approached the outer office a while ago. Heflin grew agitated and told him to back off. Much to James' relief, he did.

Observing Heflin, James sensed that the drama might be coming to an end. The computer whiz had the stance of a man who knew that his situation was hopeless.

"It's all over, isn't it?" James asked quietly.

Heflin's eyes shifted to James, who could see the signs of desperation in their depths. He had no doubt that Heflin was considering suicide. However, Patty misinterpreted the meaning of James' question to Heflin and she started to panic.

"You're going to kill us?" she shrilled. "Please! I've got children! I'm sure everybody in this room has somebody who loves them. Don't do this!"

James could feel himself react physically to Patty's words: *everybody in this room has somebody who loves them*. Unfortunately, that wasn't true in his case, but Patty needed to be there for her children. He tried to soothe her fears.

"I don't think that he's going to kill *us*."

Patty's eyes widened in horror as she began to understand what James meant. She turned to Heflin. "You're going to kill yourself?"

Heflin gave a self-depreciating snort. "Lady, I've been a dead man for quite some time."

James understood what the man meant. Divorced, in debt, and depressed, Heflin had foolishly turned one federal crime into two. But, Heflin wasn't getting any sympathy from James. Robert Heflin had decided to solve his problems by victimizing children. He deserved whatever he got. When the negotiator showed up in person a second time trying to make an attempt to persuade the abductor to release his hostages, Heflin was momentarily distracted. That's when James made his move.

****

Dana was standing across the street from the building, behind the line that the authorities set up to contain the crowd, when an officer standing nearby shouted, "Shots fired inside!"

Dana's heart nearly stopped. She gripped Sin's arm. James was listed as one of the hostages in that building! Had he been harmed? Suddenly, the disagreement which separated the two of them seemed petty when faced with the reality of the moment. All she wanted in the world was for James to walk out of the front door of the Tech Play building alive.

She began to tremble. Sin put a comforting arm around her. Glancing at him, she could see worry lines marring his handsome face.

"You like him, don't you?"

Sin shrugged. "Let's just say that he's grown on me."

Seconds ticked by, but they seemed like hours as they stood in the crowd watching the SWAT team spring into action. In full regalia, they stormed through the front doors. More time passed, and then the doors suddenly swung open and a sobbing woman was rushed out onto the street supported by several officers. A man broke through the police line and rushed toward her calling out "Patty!" The woman fell into his arms.

A few more excruciating minutes passed and a man in handcuffs was escorted out of the building. He was surrounded by a score of federal officers who hustled him into an official looking vehicle.

"That must be Heflin," Sin's jaws tightened. He kept narrowed eyes trained on the car and its passenger until it drove away.

Dana concentrated on the entrance to the building, but no one else emerged. Since shots were fired, she assumed that the medics standing by would have been summoned inside if someone was hurt, but they weren't moving. That must mean something.

"But, where's James?" she mumbled anxiously.

"He's coming out," Sin said with certainty.

The words had hardly left his mouth when James Starr's towering figure appeared in the doorway. Dana could feel the tears of relief start to flow. Without thinking, she forced her way through the police barrier and ran toward James shouting his name.

His head snapped up when he heard the voice that he had tried, unsuccessfully, to eradicate from his every waking hour. He dismissed the sound as an illusion until he saw Dana sprinting toward him with tears streaming down her face.

Forgetting every angry promise that he made to himself about not wanting to see her again, James rushed to meet her. They fell into each other's arms, and the kiss they shared declared to all that witnessed the moment that there was something special between them.

CHAPTER 31

Weeks had passed since a stranger named James Starr walked into Dana Mansfield's office. At the time neither of them would have guessed how much they would change each other's lives.

As Dana and James drove to the San Francisco airport, she reached out and lightly pinched his cheek. Surprised, James laughed heartily.

"What was that about?"

"I just wanted to make sure that you were real."

"Yeah, I'm real. We both are, and it's so good to have you here beside me."

Dana was pleased with what he said. It was a sentiment that a while ago she wasn't sure that she would ever hear from him.

Her breach of trust had been a serious barrier between them, but after his escape from Heflin they talked about it and reached an understanding. Truth and trust would be the foundation on which their relationship would be built. Without either, there was no way it could survive.

Thinking back to the day he escaped the Tech Play building, James felt that his life had been spared for a reason. He was given a second chance, and he had no intention of blowing it.

When James charged Robert Heflin, the two agents joined the fray. Caught off guard, Heflin aimed his gun directly at James who deflected the weapon just as it fired, sending the bullet into the ceiling. Putting Heflin's wrist in a death grip, James forced the gun from the culprit's hand.

"Why would you do something so foolish as to charge that man?" Dana demanded to know when she was informed of his heroics.

"Because the others had families who needed them, and I had nothing to lose."

His answer broke her heart, but her response lifted his. "You had me."

James smiled as he remembered those three words. They were like an oasis in the desert— and so was she.

When he emerged from the building to find Dana there waiting for him, they clung to each other as if the other one might disappear. It was Sin who interrupted their joyful reunion.

"I called Agent Conway and he said they were taking Heflin to the police station for questioning. I'm going down there. Do you two want to come with me?"

"I'll pass," Dana told him.

"And I've seen all of him I want to see today," James declared.

"All right, but Starr, I want you to know that you have one very satisfied customer."

"Glad to hear it." James flashed a happy grin.

The two men gave each other a hearty handshake. Sin turned to walk away, but Dana stopped him and planted a kiss on his cheek.

"Thank you."

Sin feigned confusion. "For what? All I did was pick you up from the airport." He pointed to James. "But *you* owe me."

As James took the exit that would take them to the San Francisco Airport, he was now repaying his debt. There he would proceed to the air strip reserved for the arrival and departure of private aircrafts. Sinclair's wife and two youngest children would be landing there shortly, along with Darnell, Thad and Nia.

With the capture of the trio of kidnappers, the media had resumed its frenzy, but the worse of it had died down enough for the Reasoner and Stewart families to come home. Only a few diehard media types remained at the gate to the cu-de-sac. To avoid them, the arrival home of the two families had turned into a clandestine affair. Instead of arriving at the airport on the Peninsula, they were landing at the San Francisco airport. From there they would be driven home.

Sin asked James to act as a personal bodyguard, and escort everyone back to Carmel. The plan was for James and Sin to leave the cul-de-sac disguised as Webb Starr security guards. When they arrived at the airport, a florist delivery van with darkened windows would be waiting for the families. It would be used to move everyone pass the cul-de-sac gate without raising media suspicion.

The plan hit a snag when Dana asked to come along. James objected.

"But Ray plans on meeting the family at the airport to hitch a ride to the Peninsula, and you agreed with that," she challenged.

"That's because Bev's at the Stewart house, and he wants to save himself a two hour drive. I think Ray's request is reasonable. He wants to be with his wife."

"My reason for coming along is better than his." Dana countered.

James was skeptical. "Oh, and what is that?"

"I want to be with you."

She didn't have to say anymore. Dana donned a security guard uniform, tucked her hair under the cap and passed through the gate as easily as the two men.

****

Relaxing in the back of the taxi that was taking him to the airport, Hardman reflected on the success of his trip. He wasn't a man who believed in miracles, but it seemed there was no other explanation to explain what happened to him. He didn't know what to expect when he came to the United States, but what he ended up with was more than he deserved.

His place in hell was reserved long ago. Redemption for his transgressions wasn't possible. Yet there was one good thing in his life that remained constant—his love for his family. He wanted to protect them at all costs, and he did.

Two of the bastards that hurt his love ones were behind bars. The third was in a hospital barely clinging to life. In the interim, he discovered a son who would make any man proud. He could say, without a doubt, that his work here was done.

He was on his way to catch a charter flight out of San Francisco, for the first leg of a very long journey. It was time to go home.

CHAPTER 32

Ray smiled broadly as he stood next to James and Dana inside the small terminal. They were watching the airplane piloted by her Uncle Gerald come to a stop on the tarmac. Everyone in the Stewart and Reasoner families could rest easy. Justice had been served, and they were returning home.

Ray was excited. He couldn't wait to see everyone and later join Bev in Carmel. There was no doubt that tonight's welcome home celebration would be a joyous one.

He glanced at the looming figure of James Starr, standing nearby with arms folded. He reminded Ray of a sentinel, looking every inch like a bodyguard. Nate would have been proud of his protégé. It was Nate who used to handle the investigative division of Webb Starr, but with his tragic loss, James stepped up and handled the job of finding the three kidnappers like the professional he was.

The name Webb Starr had moved center stage in the security world. James' professional success was assured. Ray's eyes slid to Dana, waiting eagerly for her family members to leave the plane. From the look of it, James' private life wasn't suffering either. The furtive glances being exchanged between James and Dana made it obvious that these two were headed for a love match. Ray was happy for them.

Inadvertently, Ray's gaze fell on a trio of men standing to his right. Their attention was trained on a small aircraft parked on the tarmac that stood ready to board its small group of passengers.

One of the men stood out. He was an older man, an African American, whose finely creased slacks and expensive shirt, didn't peg him as an average tourist. The watch that he wore was costly, and Ray knew that the price of a ticket for the chartered plane that he was about to board would be prohibitive for most people.

There was no interaction between him and the other two men who were dressed in business suits and engaged in conversation. Apparently, the man was traveling alone. Designer sunglasses were shading his eyes. Ray didn't think that he knew the stranger, yet there was something familiar about him.

Shaking off the feeling of familiarity, Ray returned his attention to the tarmac. Darnell, Thad and Nia were the first ones to exit the airplane. They were followed by Nedra and her children.

Sin was in the men's room, and hadn't returned when Dana and Ray stepped out of the small terminal to greet everyone. Simultaneously, the trio of men that had caught Ray's attention stepped outside to walk to the aircraft that was waiting for them to board.

Sensing no danger to his charges, James stayed in the terminal. This was a family reunion, and he wasn't part of the family; but if things continued with Dana the way that he hoped, who knew? Maybe one day—

He watched as the happy travelers hurried toward Ray and Dana. The smiles on the faces that he had seen in photographs and on computer screens were as bright as sunshine. He watched with special interest as the heroine herself, Gillian Reasoner, strutted with confidence toward her relatives.

Suddenly, Ray came to a stop. The others didn't seem to notice as they greeted Dana with hugs and kisses, but James was on alert. Was something wrong?

Stepping outside the terminal, his eyes swept the tarmac. Dana's uncle was at his aircraft dealing with the luggage. The only other people visible on the airstrip were the trio of men headed toward their waiting plane. One of the men had taken off his sunglasses and was observing the noisy reunion, but he kept walking, and didn't stop. He didn't appear to be a threat.

James speculated that perhaps the man recognized Darnell and Thad. Not wanting to alarm the family, James began to walk toward them when he heard footsteps behind him. He turned to see Sin trotting toward his wife and children.

Chaos reigned. Happy squeals filled the air, and another round of reunions began. James halted his steps. He couldn't help but smile at the joyful exuberance of the greetings being exchanged.

Ray remained frozen in place. The man that he noticed earlier had turned his head in his direction with his sunglasses removed. It was at that moment that Ray was no longer looking into the eyes of a stranger. He knew those eyes! He knew that face!

Years before, Ray had uncovered a secret whose existence he tried to destroy. Now the truth stood before him. There was no denying it. Those eyes and that altered face belonged to Colton Cameron. He *was* alive!

Hardman couldn't believe it. When he looked up and saw Darnell, her husband and Nia getting off of that airplane, he had to take his sun glasses off to make sure that what he was seeing was real. When Sin's wife and children appeared behind them, Hardman felt dizzy with excitement. He had to concentrate on putting one foot in front of the other and force himself to keep moving. If not, he would have collapsed.

Ray watched Bev's late husband slip his sunglasses on his face and continue walking to his aircraft. Recalling how fearful he was about what he discovered years ago about Colton Cameron's history, he knew that the man was both dangerous and deadly. It was Ray's worse nightmare that he might still be alive, and here he was in the flesh, mere steps away from his children and grandchildren. The nightmare had come true!

Despite Ray's shock and surprise it dawned on him that he felt no fear. Colton Cameron might still be breathing, but he really *was* dead. Whatever he was doing in San Francisco, it didn't matter. He could never come back to claim what he abandoned, because he no longer existed. Ray claimed the love from Bev, Darnell and Nia for himself.

Colton made choices in his life that forced him to give up everything. Except for Ray, no one would recognize him. No one would know that he still drew breath—not his wife, not his children or his grandchildren. With the death of Nathan Webb and the shredding of all evidence of the man's existence, he was as dead as he had chosen to be.

As Hardman climbed the steps on shaky legs to board the small aircraft, he looked back briefly at the children and grandchildren who he could never claim. Sin and Darnell were chatting happily, walking side by side, with their spouses.

Thad was carrying Nia on his shoulders. His youngest granddaughter was sporting a pair of stylish sunglasses, looking every inch like a miniature movie star.

The diminutive Gillian was walking in front of her parents with her arms out stretched to some man who stood waiting for the others to approach him. Hardman noted that there was confidence in every step that the little girl took. Beside her strolled his youngest grandson, seemingly oblivious to everything around him as his eyes stayed glued to his cell phone.

It seemed that Lady Luck had struck again, and Hardman was grateful. He was being presented with a moment in time that he would remember until the day he died. With that, he stepped inside of the aircraft, and the door shut behind him.

Ray stood watching his worst nightmare disappear behind closed doors. James appeared at his side.

"Is everything all right?" James looked pass him to the aircraft that had caught Ray's attention. It was moving toward the runway.

"Everything is perfect," Ray answered just as Gillian flung herself into his arms in greeting.

"Hi, Cousin Ray!" She gave him a sloppy kiss on the cheek.

"Man, am I glad we're almost home," Trevor confessed, looking up from his phone, briefly, to accept a bear hug from Ray.

"That goes for all of us," Nedra added as another round of greetings was exchanged between Ray and the rest of the family.

Gillian peeked around Ray to observe the man standing behind him. His impressive height and commanding presence demanded her attention.

"Who are you?" Her curiosity was mixed with suspicion.

Dana introduced James to her grateful family.

"We're thrilled to finally meet you in person, Mr. Starr," Darnell gave him a hug. "We'll never forget what you've done for us."

"What did he do?" Gillian wanted to know.

"This is the man who tracked down those men who took you and Nia," Sin explained.

"Oh, cool!" Trevor was impressed.

So was Gillian. "Thanks a lot!" She held her small hand out to shake James' much larger one.

"No problem, but I did it with your father's help." James gave credit where credit was due.

"All right, big brother!" Darnell flung her arms around Sin's neck, while his delighted children gave him high fives. Nedra was the only one who wasn't impressed.

"Oh, Lord, Sin, I knew that you were up to something. We're going to talk later," she threatened before turning back to James. "We'd better get home and get settled before my husband decides to sell his business and go into partnership with you."

"Oh, that's a good idea," Sin teased. He jumped back in time to miss Nedra's attempt to punch him on his arm.

As the spirited party headed to the terminal, James thought about what Nedra said. He realized that he wouldn't have any objection if Sin did want to join him. Despite his initial skepticism, the two of them made a pretty good team.

Dana read his mind. "Don't even think it," she warned. "You don't want to start World War III in the Reasoner household."

James held his hands up in surrender. "Believe me, it was just a fleeting thought."

With the others walking ahead of them, Dana and James stole a quick kiss before entering the terminal. Opening the door for her, he glanced over his shoulder at the charter plane carrying the stranger who drew his attention earlier. It was disappearing into the clouds. Dana nudged James to gain his attention.

"You know, I was just thinking, we still don't know who put that note about Robert Heflin in your mailbox."

"Unless somebody steps up to claim the reward, I guess we'll never know."

"Well, whoever it was, our family will always be grateful."

James took her hand in his. "I know what I'm grateful for."

Dana smiled up at him. "Me too."

EPILOGUE

The engagement announcement of entertainment attorney Dana Mansfield, and James Starr, CEO of Webb Starr Security Services, appeared in a copy of the *Los Angeles Times*. Identified as superstar, Darnell Cameron's aunt, as well as legal counsel, Dana's celebrity was shared with James, identified as the private investigator who tracked down the men involved in the kidnapping of the superstar's daughter and niece.

After the man in the café finished reading the brief article, he folded the newspaper neatly, withdrew a writing pen from his pocket, and placed an x on the front page, indicating that he had read this particular issue. Getting up from the table, where he had enjoyed a cup of coffee and a breakfast roll, he nodded farewell to the café owner, placed the year old newspaper back in the bin, and, with a smile on his face, walked out of the door.

THE END

DON'T MISS THE NEXT
SIN SERIES NOVEL

SHADOWS OF LOVE

NEDRA DAVIS REASONER and her sinfully sexy husband, **SINCLAIR REASONER,** have it all. Their lives are filled with love for their family, friends and their passion for each other. Nothing can tear their perfect world apart, until a shadowy figure appears in their lives and a long held secret is revealed.

The shadow is in the form of a man who has had so many names that he's not sure who he really is anymore. But, he does know *what* he is—a killer with a lot to lose.

ABOUT THE AUTHOR

Crystal V. Rhodes is an author and an award-winning playwright. Her romantic suspense novels include *Sin, Sweet Sacrifice, Sinful Intentions, Singing a Song Small Sensations, Stillwaters, Secret* and *Shadows of Love*.

Her Grandmothers, Incorporated cozy mystery series, co-written with author, L. Barnett Evans, includes the titles *Grandmothers, Incorporated* and *Saving Sin City, There's Something Wrong with Miss Zelda and Whose Knife is it Anyway?* A play based on the characters from Grandmothers, Incorporated and written by Evans and Rhodes, enjoyed a successful Off Broadway run.

Written Word Magazine named Rhodes as one of the Ten Up and Coming Authors in the Midwest. As a playwright she is the recipient of the Black Theatre Alliance Award for Best Original Writing for her stage play, *Stoops*. Rhodes has a Masters degree in Sociology and has written for newspapers, magazines, radio and television.

Visit her web site at www.crystalrhodes.com